MRS. HORNSDECKER

M.Jo

MRS. HORNSDECKER

Shawn Warren Frohmuth

iUniverse, Inc.
New York Lincoln Shanghai

Mrs. Hornsdecker

iUniverse books may be ordered through booksellers or by contacting:

iUniverse
2021 Pine Lake Road, Suite 100
Lincoln, NE 68512
www.iuniverse.com
1-800-Authors (1-800-288-4677)

ISBN-13: 978-0-595-36959-1 (pbk)
ISBN-13: 978-0-595-81368-1 (ebk)
ISBN-10: 0-595-36959-6 (pbk)
ISBN-10: 0-595-81368-2 (ebk)

Printed in the United States of America

"What seems to be the matter, Mrs. Hornsdecker?" Miss Wellsby, the librarian assistant, says as she approaches with an armful of books to be filed back onto shelves.

"Oh, this horrible computer won't let me print, nor will it let me escape from this silly Website," Bessi Hornsdecker says as she continues to press the escape key on the keyboard.

"Well, let me see if I can help," Miss Wellsby says as she places the books on the adjacent table. "This computer seems to have a mind of its own most of the time, and besides, the escape key doesn't work ever since Tommy Jones got frustrated with it," she says, pulling up another chair and sitting down.

"I have been trying to print some information about dreams from this strange Website, but the printer just won't respond," Bessi says, moving her chair over so Miss Wellsby can evaluate the problem.

"Well, it seems that this Website wants you to pay them first before you print out their material," she says as she directs the cursor using the mouse.

"That's absurd!" Bessi says as she folds her arms in front of her and shakes her head in disapproval. "I just wanted to print out a few pages—I didn't want their whole book," she says with a sigh.

"Well, it just so happens that this book arrived last week and has yet to be processed," Miss Wellsby says as she continues to close out of the Website. "If you can wait a few minutes, I'll fetch it for you."

"That would be kind of you, Miss Wellsby," Bessi says as she organizes her pieces of scratch paper on which she wrote notes about the different Websites.

"If you don't mind me asking, Mrs. Hornsdecker, what is it about dreams that you wish to research?" she asks, placing her chair back where she found it and picking up her small stack of books.

"I have been having these weird dreams and just wanted to get some non-religious opinions about what they could mean," Bessi says as she stands up and follows Miss Wellsby through the library.

"By non-religious, do you mean some other opinion than from your husband, Reverend Hornsdecker?" she asks with a smile as she places several books on the appropriate shelf.

"Yes, it seems he only has biblical answers even for a non-biblical question," Bessi says as she shuffles a few books on a shelf.

"Well, let me just put these other two books where they belong and we'll find that book about dreams for you," Miss Wellsby says as she continues to make her way through the aisle.

"I appreciate you spending the time to do this, Miss Wellsby. You must have a ton of the things to do before closing for the evening," Bessi says, following Miss Wellsby into the back room of the library.

"Actually, Mrs. Hornsdecker, the library officially closed twenty minutes ago, but I have a few more things to do before I can close up here," she says, approaching a large table of books recently unpackaged.

"Oh my, I am so sorry to keep you then. I had no idea I was on that computer for so long," Bessi says as she picks up one of the new books from the table.

"It is easy to lose track of time when searching for something on the Internet," Miss Wellsby says as she looks through several of the books on the table. "Besides, I don't mind in the least staying a little late to help you find a book that may help you with your dreams. Oh, here it is," she says as she removes some advertisement inserts from within the book's cover. "The book is titled *Dreams: The Untold Story*," she says, handing the book to Bessi.

"Oh, I just don't know how I could thank you for taking the trouble to help me like this," Bessi says as she opens the book and glances at a few of the pages.

"Just return it undamaged and without anyone knowing that you got it from the library with out checking it out," Miss Wellsby says with a smile.

"Thank you so much. I'll return it as soon as I have read it," Bessi says with a smile as she begins to walk out of the room and through the library with Miss Wellsby.

"Maybe we can spend some time discussing the book when you are finished reading it," Miss Wellsby says as she opens the front door for Bessi.

"I would like that," Bessi says as she exits. "Thank you again, Miss Wellsby, and good night."

"Good night, Mrs. Hornsdecker and say hello to your husband and your twins for me," Miss Wellsby says.

"Thank you. I will do that," Bessi says as she continues down the library steps to her car.

After several minutes, Bessi arrives at the local grocery store owned by one of her best friends, Iona Williams.

"Hello, Iona, how is business today?" she asks, picking up a small shopping basket.

"Oh, hello there, Bessi," Iona says as she rings up items for Mrs. Higgins. "Business is as usual."

"Well hello, Mrs. Hornsdecker," Mrs. Higgins says as she hands Iona the money for her groceries. "How is your family?"

"Fine, thank you, Mrs. Higgins, and how are your daughter's piano lessons coming along?" Bessi asks as she smiles at Iona.

"Martha keeps playing every day and her instructor says she has great potential," Mrs. Higgins says as she receives her change from Iona. "Well, have a good evening," she says as she grabs her bag of groceries and exits the store.

"One of this town's least interesting people, I would have to say," Iona says to Bessi as she wipes the countertop with a folded damp towel. "Are you still having those bothersome dreams dear?" she asks, walking back to the vegetable section of her small store.

"Yes, and I wish they would end," Bessi says as she picks through the ears of corn. "Miss Wellsby loaned me a book on dreams and I hope it helps," she says, picking out a head of lettuce and looking over at Iona with a sigh.

"You poor dear, I don't know what I would do If I was having those dreams of yours," Iona says, repositioning several potatoes. "My lettuce and corn wouldn't be fresh, that's for sure," she says with a chuckle and a smile to Bessi, who smiles back.

"You are such a dear to always lend me an ear," she says as she begins walking back to the front of the store.

"What are friends for, right?" Iona says as she starts to place some of the vegetables on the scale and others in a plastic bag. "Are you still going to be able to join the group this Saturday at Thelma's?" she says as she rings up the groceries.

"Tired or not, I wouldn't miss stitching those last quilt panels for our community project," Bessi says as she hands Iona some money for the groceries.

"I almost have my panel finished and I am as excited as you to finally get that thing connected with the rest of them," Iona says, handing Bessi some change. "You have a great night's sleep and give my best to the family," Iona says with a smile.

"Thank you, Iona. You are a dear friend," Bessi says as she begins to exit the store. "See you Saturday."

"See you Saturday," Iona says as she wipes off the counter with a damp towel. Then she watches Bessi drive out of the parking lot and down the street.

Several miles pass and Bessi arrives home. Her daughter, Louisa, greets her at the door and helps her with the grocery bag. "Hello, Mom, how was your day?" Louisa asks with a kiss and a smile.

"Fine, dear, and how was your day at school?" Bessi says as she places her purse and book on the entry table.

"Just another day at high school, Mom," Louisa says, taking the groceries into the kitchen where her twin brother Lewis is trying to fix the drain under the kitchen sink.

"Hi, Mom," Lewis says, sliding out from under the sink.

"What are you doing to the sink drain?" Bessi says as she starts to pull the vegetables from the grocery bag. "Am I going to be able to use the sink to prepare dinner?" she asks with a smile.

"Sure, Mom," Lewis says, grabbing the pipe wrench from the countertop. "Dad caught his tie clip on something and it dropped into the sink. I'll have it put back together in a moment, Mom," Lewis says, scooting back under the sink.

"You are so helpful, Lewis. How I got so lucky to have such wonderful children, I'll probably never know," Bessi says, pulling out a pot and pan from the cupboard. "Where is your father, by the way?" she asks, putting on her kitchen apron.

Louisa enters the room with a sheet of paper, "Dad had to go out to the Cransford's farm to help Mr. Cransford with his injured horse," She says, handing her mother the sheet of paper.

"What is this dear?" Bessi asks as she holds the paper.

"It's a consent form for us to be in this year's senior graduation play. Mrs. Barnsworth wants this year's play to be in honor of the townspeople who donated the money to build our new gymnasium," Louisa says, kneeling down next to her brother. "Are you sure you know what you are doing?" she asks with a smile.

"No, but I am learning," Lewis says with a chuckle.

"What?" Bessi replies with a chuckle. "We need that sink to prepare dinner, mister," she says with a chuckle.

"I'll have it ready in a few more minutes, Mom," Lewis says.

"What a nice idea, to have the play in honor of the donors," Bessi says as she leans on the counter reading the form.

"We have not picked out the play yet, Mom. Our teacher says that the graduating class will have to agree on a play before the first of the month.," Louisa says. "And, whatever play we do choose, it has to have enough parts in it to include the entire class," Louisa says as she walks over to stand next to her mother.

"How many students are in your senior class?" Bessi asks as she walks over to the sink.

"Twenty-seven students," Lewis says sliding out from under the sink. "And the sink is back in working condition," he says, turning on the water faucet and looking back under the sink for any leaks.

"Twenty-seven students will be a large cast for a play," Bessi says as she begins to fill one of the pots with water for the corn that Louisa is already shucking.

"Maybe the play can have a bunch of inanimate objects like trees or rocks or something," Louisa says with a chuckle.

"Well, that wouldn't be any fun," Bessi says as she places the lettuce in the sink to wash it. "I am sure you all can come up with some wonderful play to perform and have fun doing."

"I hope it's going to be a love story," Louisa says as she places the ears of corn in the sink for washing.

"Not me. I hope it has knights and dragons with a damsel in distress," Lewis says as he closes the sink cabinet. "There, all done."

"Good work, honey," Bessi kisses Lewis on the forehead. "Did you find your father's tie clip?"

"Yeah, he won't like to know what else was in the drain along with it, though," Lewis says with a chuckle.

"What do you mean?" Louisa asks.

"I mean that there is lots of grime in that drain," Lewis says. "And it is gross."

"Well, please be sure to wash your hands, OK?," Bessi says as she watches Lewis exit the kitchen through the backdoor, heading to the garage to return the tools to the toolbox. "That brother of yours is very special, you know," she says, kissing Louisa on the forehead. "And so are you, dear."

"Thanks, Mom," Louisa says as she leaves the kitchen. "I'm going up to my room to try and think of some ideas for the play."

"OK, dear, I'll call you when dinner's ready," Bessi says as she finishes washing the lettuce. "Oh, Lewis, by the way, when did your father say he was getting back from the Cransford's?"

"He didn't say, Mom, but I can call the farm and check on him," Lewis says as he returns to the kitchen.

"That would be nice, dear, but first, please wash those hands of yours," Bessi says with a smile.

"OK, Mom," Lewis says, exiting the kitchen.

A little time passes and Lewis returns to the kitchen, "Mom, I called Mr. Cransford and he says Dad is on his way home."

"Great, perfect timing because dinner will be ready in about fifteen minutes," Bessi says as she places the corn in boiling water.

"Did you have another strange dream again last night, Mom?" Lewis asks as he takes several of the salad plates to the dinner table.

"Yes, I did, and, thank you for asking, Lewis," Bessi says as she stirs something in a pan on the stove.

"What does Dad think about your dreams?" Lewis asks as he places the remaining salad plates on the table.

"He doesn't really have an explanation for them," Bessi says, pulling out silverware from a drawer.

"Maybe God is trying to communicate to you through your dreams, Mom," Lewis suggests beginning to fill the water glasses from the automatic water dispenser on the refrigerator door.

"If that is the case, I just wish there could be a clearer channel of communication between us that was not so symbolic and confusing."

"Dad is home!" Louisa says as she comes down the stairs.

A tall bearded man comes in the house through the front door.

"Hello everybody. Sorry I am late," he says as he hangs his jacket in the hall closet.

"How is Mr. Cransford's horse, Father?" Lewis asks as he enters the hall from the kitchen.

"His legs are torn up something horrible, but he is all right," Silus says as he enters the kitchen.

"Well, hello there, Mr. Veterinarian," Bessi says as she kisses her husband on the cheek with a wooden spoon in her hand. "Dinner will be ready shortly."

"Great, I am starving," Silus says as he exits the kitchen. "I'll just get cleaned up and check my message machine in the office."

"I'll have one of the kids call when the food is on the table," Bessi says, taking off her apron and hanging it in the kitchen pantry. After wiping down the counter next to the sink, she sets the stove's burner to simmer and the timer for six minutes. Bessi exits the kitchen for a moment and then returns with the dream book she got from Miss Wellsby.

"What are you reading, Mom?" Lewis asks, entering the kitchen with an empty water glass from his room.

"Its called *Dreams: The Untold Story*," she says with a smile. "Miss Wellsby at the library just received the book and said I could borrow it."

"I didn't know you had a library card, Mom?" Lewis says, placing the glass in the dishwasher.

"I don't, dear. She loaned it to me from the library's new arrivals," Bessi says, thumbing through the index pages of the book. "Don't tell anyone that she loaned it to me before the library had the chance to add it to their catalog, OK?"

"OK, Mom," Lewis says with a chuckle as he exits the room and the timer goes chimes. "I'll tell Louisa and Dad that dinner is ready."

"Thank you, dear," Bessi says as she turns off the stove's burner and pulls out a serving plate. After placing all the food on the table, Louisa is the first to arrive, "Smells great, Mom. What is it?" she asks, sitting in her usual seat.

"Tofu surprise. Soy tofu and red wild rice, mushrooms and pearl onions. On the side, we are having corn on the cob and a green salad," Bessi says with a proud sigh as she looks at the table all decorated with dinner items.

"Whatever it is, Mom, it sure smells great," Lewis says, entering and taking his seat. "Dad says he'll be down in a few minutes. He said the Holcomb family had domestic questions that he wants to answer."

"Oh well, their family does have more problems than other families," Bessi says as she sits down at the table.

"Sorry to be late, dear," Silus says as he kisses Bessi on the head and sits at the head of the table. "Wow, this looks great, honey," he says, loading up his plate.

"Mom calls it her tofu surprise," Louisa says as she begins to load her plate with the food.

"How were your dreams last night, Mom?" Lewis says as he loads his plate with the tofu dish.

"Well, another weird sequence of dreams that really concern me," Bessi says as she dishes up her plate.

"Oh, those dreams are just your active imagination, dear. You shouldn't be getting all upset over them," Silus says as he places his hand on his wife's arm. "They are just dreams, honey."

"You think that they are just dreams but they are not, Silus. You continue to try and shrug my dreams off as something unimportant, but they are very important to me," Bessi says, placing her hands on her forehead for a few seconds.

"Mom, don't get upset. Maybe they will pass soon," Louisa says, taking a piece of corn from a bowl.

"Yes, and maybe they won't, either," Bessi says with a smile. "I just wish I didn't dream at all."

"I wish I could remember my dreams, Mom," Lewis says, taking a piece of corn and placing it on his plate.

"Dreams are just our subconscious trying to act out some element of our life," Silus says as he begins to eat his meal. "I wish you wouldn't get so wrapped up in them, dear."

"I can't help it. You try waking up every night with some strange memory of some weird group of people in some weird world," Bessi says, beginning to eat her meal. "It would be different if it were not every night, and also two, three or four times a night," she says with a smile to Louisa and Lewis.

"Have you considered talking to your doctor about the dreams, Mom?" Louisa says as she takes another bite of the tofu dish.

"Your mother doesn't need any doctor to tell her about her dreams. She needs to not be so stressed out over them and they will just probably go away," Silus says, taking a drink of water. "Or, you could try praying a little more often and let God heal your mind," he says, continuing to eat.

"Sometimes God can't solve all things, Silus," Bessi says, putting down her fork and lifting her water glass. "Sometimes there are things that go on in life that may have nothing to do with God," she says, taking a drink of water.

"Honey, you don't need to say such things in front of the kids," Silus says with a disapproving sigh.

"I'm sorry, kids. I didn't mean anything against God. I was just trying to express that there are things in a person's life that God may not be part of," she says, continuing to eat.

"I understand, Mom," Lewis says, continuing to eat.

"I understand too, Mom," Louisa says as she drinks some water then begins eating her corn on the cob.

"Well, I'll add some special prayers tomorrow, dear, and we'll see if that can at least help," Silus says as he finishes his meal. "That was delicious, Bessi. Now if you all don't mind, I want to go into the office and see if there is something in my religious references that may shed some light on this dream issue."

"Oh, Silus, you don't need to go and do that," Bessi says, folding her napkin.

"I am just trying to help," Silus says as he stands and exits the room.

"What was your dream last night, Mom?" Louisa says as she begins to clear the table.

"Oh, you'll just think it is silly like your father," Bessi says as she picks up several plates and takes them into the kitchen.

"Mom, come on, tell us," Lewis says as he brings several of the drinking glasses into the kitchen. "We don't agree with Dad about your dreams," he says, returning to the table for more glasses.

"All right, as soon as we clean up the dinner dishes, we'll sit down and I'll tell you my dream," Bessi says, running the dishwater in the sink.

"Great, I'll rinse and you dry, Lewis," Louisa says as she gets out several towels from a drawer and sets them on the counter.

Within a few minutes, the dishes were rinsed, then dried, and put away.

"Well, that doesn't take too long when we all work together," Lewis says as he hangs his towel on the stove's handle.

"Well, let's go into the living room and I'll tell you both about my dreams last night," Bessi says, exiting the room with Louisa and Lewis following her.

In the living room, Bessi sits on the couch and begins to explain her dreams. "I first remember being in a tall pine tree with a warm breeze teasing the needles. Then I realized that I was hanging from a branch by my hands and a green pig suddenly appeared introducing himself as your father. He asked me to lift up my feet and he would swing me out into the soft pine needles. I don't know why I trusted him, but I did. I lifted up my legs and he clamped onto my ankles. He told me to let go of the branch and I did. As I fell backward, the warm air soothed me and for a moment I felt light and free. Then, suddenly the green pig let go of my feet and I began to fall. I kept falling through the branches until I woke," Bessi says, shrugging her shoulders and looking at Lewis who just stared at her.

"I wish I had dreams like that, Mom," Lewis says.

"Me too, except for the falling part," Louisa says as she hugs her mother's arm. "No wonder you're so upset about your dreams."

"Yeah, really, Mom," Lewis says. "Especially when the green pig says he is Dad."

"It was strange," Bessi says as she leans back into the couch. "The next dream is even weirder. I couldn't fall back asleep for over an hour, but finally did. I first remember being in a crowd of people that I have never met. The crowd was slowly moving toward some kind of bright pulsating light. I could stop from moving with the crowd. It was almost like I was being drawn toward the light like a magnet that slowly pulls a piece of metal toward it. Then, in front of me I could see people beginning to change into liquid-like forms that began to crawl and wiggle. But, some of the people were turning into bright lights with part of their human form surrounded by rays of sunlight. Those people were lifting up into the sun. The people crawling were making weird noises and crying for help. I kept getting closer to the light and began to panic, wondering if I was to become part of the light or one of those creatures. I woke very scared and confused and had to turn the light on," Bessi says, holding her hand over her mouth as she closes her eyes.

"Mom, no wonder you are having such a horrible time about your dreams," Louisa says. "If I had that dream, I would be hysterical."

"If I had that dream, I would be in a psych unit," Lewis says as he shakes his head and shoulders.

"Before you get our children any more startled and upset over your dreams, shouldn't we all get ready for bed?" Silus asks from the entry hallway where he had been listening.

"I hope you don't have any more of those dreams tonight, Mom," Lewis says as he kisses her on the cheek.

"Mom, if you do have any more weird dreams, wake me up and I'll sit with you, OK?" Louisa says, kissing her mother on her other cheek.

"Good night, Dad," Lewis says, passing Silus in the doorway.

"Good night, Daddy," Louisa says, giving him a kiss on the cheek and going upstairs to her room.

"Honey, you shouldn't tell the kids about those weird dreams, especially just before they go to bed," Silus says as he sits down next to Bessi. "I didn't find anything of help in my references here at home, but tomorrow I'll check in my office at the church. I am sure I'll find some explanation for what you are experiencing," Silus says as he kisses Bessi on the cheek. "Let's go on up to bed, OK?"

"All right, just let me do a few things in the kitchen and I'll be upstairs shortly," Bessi says as she stands and walks to the kitchen. On her way to the staircase, she stops to get the book Miss Wellsby loaned her and she walks slowly up stairs while she glances through the book's index.

"What is that?" Silus asks as he slips on his pajama top and folds back the bedspread.

"It is a book Miss Wellsby loaned me about dreams," Bessi says, setting it down on her nightstand. "I tried getting some information from the Internet on the library's computer, but I had trouble getting access. Miss Wellsby just happened to have this book about dreams," Bessi says as she steps into her dressing room to change into her nightgown.

"*Dreams: The Untold Story*," Silus reads the title of the book. "Honey, I hope you are not going to get involved in some dream fanaticism just because you have a few weird dreams," he says, thumbing through the book.

"I just want some one else's opinion about what dreams may mean. That's all," Bessi says as she slips into bed and gently reaches for her book.

"As you wish, dear. I just hope it doesn't add to your dream paranoia," Silus says as he kisses her on the forehead and then turns over covering his shoulder with the blankets.

"I won't have the light on long, dear. I just want to glance through the book before I go to bed," Bessi says, sinking down into her pillows as she begins to read her book.

After an hour, she turns the light off and goes to sleep.

She suddenly wakes, "Oh my gosh!" Bessi says as she sits up in bed. She turns toward the clock to see it is only three in the morning and she sighs. "Will these dreams ever end?" she asks softly getting up from the bed and exiting the room. As she walks down the stairs, several small creaks in the wood slow her pace. "Why do I have to have these dreams every night?" she asks herself. "Tonight I was sailing with a person I have never met. I have never been sailing before in my life. Yet, there we were," she says as she enters the living room where she turns on a light and sits in a chair with her book.

The first person up is Louisa. "Mom, did you have another bad dream last night?" she asks, entering the living room.

"Well, let's say it was weird, not to mention scary," Bessi says, closing her book and yawning.

"What happened?" Louisa asks as she hugs her Mom.

"I'll tell you later, dear, OK? I don't want this to be on your mind today. You have too much to think about at school," Bessi says, standing. "I'll start getting breakfast ready."

"OK, Mom," Louisa says as she glances at the book on the table next to the chair. "I'll get ready for school," she says, setting the book down and leaving the room.

"Good morning, dear," Silus says as he kisses Bessi on the forehead in the kitchen. "Did you have another bad dream last night?" he asks, pouring himself a cup of coffee.

"Yes, it was weird and I'll tell you about it later," Bessi says, putting several boxes of cereal on the table.

"What time did you get up?" Silus asks as he walks to the edge of the kitchen.

"I think it was about three this morning," Bessi says as she places silverware and bowls on the table.

"Well, try and get a nap in today," Silus says as he leaves the room. "I'll be down shortly."

"OK," Bessi says, pouring herself a cup of coffee.

"Good morning, Mom," Lewis says as he kisses his Mom on the cheek. "Did you sleep better last night?"

"Not really. I had another weird dream that I will tell you about later," Bessi says, pouring Lewis a glass of orange-banana juice.

"All right, Mom. I have to run this morning. Some of the guys on the track team are starting to train earlier before the girls start taking over the inside lane," Lewis says, sitting down and pouring some cereal.

"Why do the girls just want the inside lane of the track?" Bessi asks as she sits next to Lewis.

"Ask Louisa," Lewis says, taking a bite of cereal.

"What does she have to do with it?" Bessi asks.

"Some of the guys think she is one of several girls who want to prove to the guys that they are equal in everything that we do. So, they try and participate in whatever activity we are doing," Lewis says, taking another bite of cereal.

"That's funny," Bessi says. "But, it is surely harmless."

"Yes, I guess nothing will come of it. Most of the guys are attracted to the girls so they just go along with it," Lewis says, drinking his milk from his bowl.

"You eat too fast young man," Bessi says, standing and going to the kitchen counter. "Here is your lunch. We ran out of sandwich meat so you have peanut butter and jelly, all right?" she asks, handing Lewis his lunch bag.

"As long as it is made with your homemade grape jelly," Lewis says as he kisses his Mom on the cheek and takes his lunch. "See you after school, Mom, love you."

"Love you too, dear," Bessi says, pouring herself some fresh coffee and sitting back down at the table.

"I have to run early, Mom," Louisa says as she quickly enters into the room and sits at the table. "Did Lewis already leave for school?"

"Yes, he did, and he says you and several other girls are competing for the inside lane of the school's track," she says with a smile.

"Well, at least he didn't exaggerate the situation," Louisa says as she pours some cereal. "We just feel that some of us can run just as fast as they can and we intend to prove it," she says, drinking some of her juice. "Great juice flavor, Mom."

"Thank you, dear. I took the rest of the bananas and blended them in with the frozen orange concentrate," Bessi says, seeing Silus enter the room dressed in his suit.

"Good morning, Daddy," Louisa says, getting a kiss on the top of her head from her father.

"Good morning, honey bunky, and good morning again to you, dear," Silus says as he sits down and pours some cereal into a bowl. "I'll have to run off quickly this morning, dear. I have a few things to do at the church before the flock begin arriving," he says, pouring milk over his cereal.

"Is the church still going to have the fundraiser next month?" Louisa asks, drinking some of her coffee.

"It all depends on if we get enough volunteers," Silus says as he finishes his coffee and begins eating.

"Would you care for more coffee, dear?" Bessi asks.

"Not this morning, Bessi. I think this is going to be a one-cup morning," Silus says, eating his cereal.

"Well, I have to run, Mom. Hope your day goes well," Louisa says, taking her bowl to the sink and then grabbing her lunch bag.

"I made you peanut butter and jelly today. I hope that is all right," Bessi says with a smile.

"That is perfect, Mom. I hope it is with some of your homemade jam," Louisa says as she kisses her Mom on the cheek and then goes over and kisses he father's cheek. "See you both after school," she says leaving the house through the front door.

"We are lucky to have such great kids," Bessi says with a smile.

"You are right. We are very lucky. And, I am luckier to have a wife like you," Silus says as he leaves his chair and kisses Bessi. "I need to be on my way, dear. If you need me and I am not at the church, I'll be down at the barber shop getting a trim," he says, grabbing his briefcase, leaving the room with Bessi right behind him.

"Well, I hope you have a great day, dear," Bessi says, kissing and hugging Silus.

"OK, and later you'll tell me about your dream?" Silus asks as he opens the front door.

"Yes, dear," Bessi says with a smile as she waves to Silus walking down the steps.

Bessi closes the door and returns to the table where she finishes her coffee and then cleans up the kitchen. After one last cup of coffee, she returns to her room where she takes a two-hour nap.

The phone rings and Bessi reaches for the bedside table as she places her dream book next to the phone and picks up the receiver. "Hello."

"Hello Bessi. This is Thelma. Are you going to make it to tea today?" Thelma asks.

"Oh, is that today?" Bessi says, holding the phone as she stretches out her other arm and yawns. "Yes, of course, dear. I'll be over."

"If you can make it here by noon, I would love for you to give me some advice on my iris patch before tea starts," Thelma says.

"Sure, I would love to, dear," Bessi says as she sits up in bed. "I'll see you around noon, OK?"

"OK, dear. Bye for now," Thelma says, hanging up the phone.

"I wonder how long I slept?" Bessi asks, hanging up the phone and glancing at the clock. "Two and a half hours, great goodness!" she says, getting out of bed and heading to the bathroom to turn on the shower. "The day will be over before I even get dressed."

Hearing the phone ring she picks up the receiver near the walk-in closet, "Hello."

"Hello, dear. It's Phoebe. Are you going to tea and knitting today?" Phoebe asks.

"Yes, and I'll be a little early. Thelma has some questions about her iris patch," Bessi says as she stretches the phone cord to turn the water off.

"Oh yes, it seems she has a master gardener at work with two very large front teeth and an appetite to go with them," Phoebe says with a chuckle.

"You mean that horrible old gopher is back in her yard again?" Bessi says with disapproving sounds.

"Yes, it seems to be that old gray critter that only eats her purple iris and never the yellow or blue ones," Phoebe says, laughing.

"It seems impossible for a gopher to be able to identify an iris color by its roots and have a taste for that color over any other color," Bessi says with disbelief.

"Well, dear, I'll be there a bit early myself. I just have got to see this," Phoebe says.

"You and me both. I'll see you there then. Bye," Bessi says, hanging up the phone and turning the shower on again. "It sounds insane that an old gopher would have a preference for purple irises," she says, stepping into the shower and adjusting the water's temperature.

After showering and getting dressed, Bessi finishes cleaning the kitchen and heads off to do some errands. She first stops by the school and drops off the consent form for Louisa and Lewis to be in the school's senior play. Then she picks up the dry cleaning and drops off Silus' lunch at the church.

While at the church, she doesn't find her husband and is told that he is down at the barbershop for a haircut. Bessi then goes into the church and says a small prayer about her dreams. Then she goes to visit Harriet Nimmo, one of her best friends, who runs the local retirement home.

"Hi there, could you please tell me where I could find Harriet?" Bessi asks one of the nurses she knows on a friendly basis.

"Oh hello, Mrs. Hornsdecker," the nurse says with a smile. "Mrs. Nimmo is in the north garden with several of the local gardeners.

"Thank you, nurse," Bessi says as she makes her way to the north garden where she finds Harriet.

"Oh hello, dear," Harriet says with a warm hug and kiss to the cheek. "How are you sleeping these days? Are you still having those weird dreams?" Harriet asks as she waves the gardeners on.

"Yes, I am afraid they are getting worse too." Bessi says as she sits down on a garden chair with Harriet. "Miss Wellsby loaned me a book on dreams that I am slowly reading, but I don't think I'll get any answers to what the dreams mean, only a few ideas about why they might be happening."

"Well, it is a popular belief among specialists that dreams are our subconscious trying to teach us things or explain things about ourselves that we don't yet understand," Harriet says, waving at a groundskeeper to bring them something to drink.

"If my subconscious is trying to tell me something, then why doesn't it just come right out and tell me rather than go through all this symbolism," Bessi says, pulling out a handkerchief from her skirt pocket.

"I wish I could answer that for you, dear," Harriet says with a comforting gesture. "But, it is out of my league," she says, seeing the nurse's aide bringing two glasses of lemonade. "What did you dream last night?" she asks and then thanks the aide for the drink.

"Last night, I was sailing with this person. I think it might have been my husband, but I am not certain. Anyway, we were sailing and I was pulling in a net full of dishes that the fish had picked clean. Then suddenly we were stuck on this sandbar and the sails became limp and were flapping. The other person tied the sails down and then jumped into the water. After swimming a few feet, the person walked out of the water onto a small beach with a tree planted in the middle. The person began collecting things broken by the waves and counting them. As this person collected more and more things, the island became covered with all these objects and the person started to merge with the objects. Suddenly, the boat began to drift away and all I could do is stand watching. The person then became larger and larger as the plastic-like objects collected. The person became a hideous monster with all kinds of strange noises and bodily fluids pouring out from this abstract form," Bessi says, lightly weeping.

"Oh, dear," Harriet says, patting Bessi's knee. "You are having some strange dreams."

"I woke up not even realizing where I was and who I was sleeping next to," Bessi says, looking out into the garden where the gardeners prune vegetation.

"Have you thought about going to see your doctor and ask what he has to think of all these dreams?" Harriet asks.

"No, he would think I was going crazy or something," Bessi says with a smile.

"Or, maybe he could prescribe something that would make the dreams stop," Harriet says as she takes another sip of her lemonade.

"If this persists, I'll have no choice but to discuss the situation with my doctor, but for now, just being able to talk to my friends about the dreams helps tremendously," Bessi says as she takes a drink of her lemonade. "Good lemonade, Harriet."

"Thank you, dear. I picked the lemons from the west garden this morning and made it myself with my grandmother's recipe," Harriet says with a smile. "I am sorry you are having these weird dreams and wish that there was something I could do for you."

"Thank you, Harriet, but I'll just have to hope that they will stop soon and I can get back to a normal life," Bessi says with a smile. She then finishes her drink and gets up to leave. "I need to be on my way, but thank you for letting me talk. Harriet, you're one of my best friends," she says, hugging Harriet and kissing her on the cheek.

"Thank you, dear. You are my best friend," Harriet says, turning and walking with Bessi to her car. "I won't be joining the group today for tea I have too much to do, training the gardeners to prune things my way," Harriet says with a chuckle and a smile. "You take care, dear, and if I don't talk to you later today, you'll hear from me tomorrow, OK?"

"OK, thank you, again," Bessi says as she waves and then turns to walk across the mowed lawn to her car. "I wonder if I shouldn't stop by my doctor's office and set up an appointment?" she says to herself. "It's only ten thirty and I am not due at Thelma's for another half-hour. So why not?" she says, pulling out of the parking lot and slowly making her way along the winding driveway surrounded by lawns, gardens, and old well-groomed trees.

Half-way through town, Bessi pulls into the hospital parking lot and finds a spot next to the school's coach who was just getting ready to leave.

"Well, hello there, Mrs. Hornsdecker," Mr. Strickle says as he opens his car door. "What brings you to the hospital?"

"Oh, I'm just parking here. I am actually just going into Dr. Sackert's office to make a checkup appointment," Bessi says as she closes her car door and walks around her vehicle toward Mr. Strickle.

"Well, I had to have my annual prostate cancer testing here in the hospital today," Mr. Strickle says with a half-smile.

"How is your treatment coming along, Mr. Strickle?" Bessi asks with sympathy.

"Well, they tell me it's not progressing so I keep doing whatever they say to do," Mr. Strickle says as he waves to Bessi. "I need to get back to the school now, but it was nice to talk with you."

"Thank you, Mr. Strickle. You take care now," Bessi says as she turns and continues walking to the doctor's office.

"Hello, Mrs. Hornsdecker," the receptionist says as Bessi enters the waiting room.

"Hello, Kate. I would like to make a general checkup appointment with Dr. Sackert, please," Bessi says, looking a little pre-occupied.

"Is there anything wrong, Mrs. Hornsdecker?" Kate asks.

"No, no. I just want to get a checkup and ask a few questions, that's all," Bessi says, looking around the room of the empty waiting area.

"OK, Dr. Sackert can see you next Wednesday at ten thirty in the morning. Would that work for you?" Kate asks with a smile.

"That would be fine, dear," Bessi says as she reaches for the appointment card that Kate hands her. "Thank you, and I'll see you then," Bessi says as she exits the waiting room and Kate picks up an incoming call.

Bessi gets to her car and is greeted by another acquaintance. After several neighborly words, she drives off toward Thelma's house for her bi-weekly tea and knitting group.

"Hello, Bessi dear," Thelma says from a flowerbed as Bessi pulls into the driveway.

"Just another day in the world," Bessi says, stepping out of the car and walking over to the dahlia flowerbed.

"Oh, but a beautiful day it is indeed," Thelma says, stepping through the flowers over to Bessi and then gives her a hug and kiss on the cheek.

"I wish I had your outlook on things, Thelma," Bessi says with a sigh.

"Well, get those dreams under control and you will dear," Thelma says, looking back onto the flowerbed. "I wouldn't mind as much if that old gray gopher would eat some of these bulbs instead of insisting on my purple iris from Venice," she says waving her hands with frustration.

"I have been giving the issue some thought and I think I might have an answer to that problem," Bessi says, beginning to walk with Thelma toward the iris patch beside the garage.

"Well, if anyone can figure it out, dear, it will be you," Thelma says, pointing at the gopher damage in her iris patch. "See what that old goober is doing. I have a mind to feed him something that will put more than gray hair on his head," she says with a smile. "But, I don't dare harm him. He's been around since my husband Arlo died and I just couldn't harm the critter."

"Thelma, do you remember when you had the two stray cats that moved into your garage?" Bessi asks, stepping over to the edge of the iris patch.

"Yes, I do. They found their way into the garage through a hole in the wire that covered the air vent," Thelma says, looking over to Bessi.

"If I remember right, Arlo use to feed the cats at the edge of the garage. Did he not?" Bessi asks with a smile.

"A matter of fact, he did. What has that to do with this old bucktoothed iris eater?" Thelma says with a smile.

"I remember being over her several times and seeing Arlo tossing stale dry cat food into this area when he wanted the cats to have fresh food," Bessi says with an inquisitive tilt of her head.

"Yes, he did. It used to bug me when he would waste all that food," Thelma says with a shake of her head.

"My dear friend, maybe what has happened is that the purple iris have taken on some of the cat food flavor from the soil and that old gopher has acquired a taste for them," Bessi says with a smile.

"Oh heavens. You know, Bessi dear, I think you're right," Thelma says, putting her hand over her mouth. "I should have thought about that. With your clever mind, you have figured it out," Thelma says with a chuckle.

"It is just a possibility," Bessi says with a smile. "Years of dry cat food being put into the soil might just make whatever you grow there taste like cat food."

"It is more than a possibility. It has to be what has happened. That makes perfect sense, dear," Thelma says, hugging Bessi from the side. "I wish I had half of your perceptive abilities, Bessi."

"I wonder what we could do about it, Thelma," Bessi says, kneeling down and taking some of the soil into her hands.

"I think I'll have to transplant every one of those irises out of this area and plant something like garlic or onions until the old fart dies of heartburn," Thelma says with a chuckle.

"Where would you move all those irises too?" Bessi asks

"I'll have one of the gardeners till up some of the lawn and I'll plant them there," Thelma says with a shrug of her shoulders.

"What about, for now, just trying to put out some cat food to fill him up so he doesn't eat any more of the irises," Bessi says.

"That is a good idea. I don't want to disturb these plants until after the iris show next spring," Thelma says. "Oh, what would I do without you Bessi?" Thelma asks as she steps over to the entrance of the house.

"I'll pull out the quilt panels from the wood trunk and start getting ready," Bessi says as she enters the house.

"OK, I'll just get cleaned up and set out the tea platter," Thelma says. "And maybe we'll have time before the others get you to talk about some of your dreams," she says, heading to the kitchen while Bessi heads off to the knitting room across the hall from the library. The doorbell then rings.

"Could you get that, Bessi? I'm on a stool trying to get something down from the upper cupboards," Thelma calls out from with in the kitchen.

"Sure, dear," Bessi says as she answers the door. "Hello, Phoebe. How are you doing, dear?"

"Oh just fine. I should be asking you how you are," Phoebe says as she kisses Bessi on the cheek and gives her a light hug.

"Well, under the circumstances, I am doing fine," Bessi says, closing the door and returning to the knitting room to prepare for the meeting.

"Phoebe, is that you dear?" Thelma asks from the kitchen.

"Yes, Thelma," Phoebe answers with a smile to Bessi.

"Could you please lend me a hand for a second, please?" Thelma asks.

"Certainly dear. Oh my, what are you doing on that stool?" Pheobe asks as she enters the kitchen.

"Can I hand you this platter and serving set?" Thelma asks.

"Well, of course. You be careful up there. Even though it is only three feet up, it would be quite a fall at your age," Phoebe says with a smile.

"Thank you, dear," Thelma says, handing down a large silver platter. "Just put this on to the counter and I'll have to dust it off."

"What's wrong with the old one we always use?" Phoebe asks.

"That one is off being polished and engraved," Thelma says, handing down a wooden box of serving utensils.

"Engraved?" Phoebe asks, taking the box and setting it on the counter. The doorbell rings again.

"Yes, I thought I would donate that old platter to the school's fundraiser this year. It has more history than you and I put together," Thelma says laughing.

"Well, that says a lot for its history, doesn't it?" Phoebe says as she turns to go answer the doorbell.

"Thank you, dear. I can manage, now, if you can accompany everyone to the knitting room," Thelma says, stepping down from the stool.

"It's Tessa!" Phoebe calls out as she greets her with a half-hug and kiss to the cheek. "Hello, dear."

"Hello, hello, hello, and as Bessi always says, here we are, another day in the world."

"And a good day at that," Phoebe says as she closes the door and follows Tessa to the knitting room.

"And how is our dreamer doing these days?" Tessa asks as she greats Bessi with a half-hug and a kiss to the cheek.

"Survived another night of dreams and looking forward to getting this quilt finished soon," Bessi says as she sets out different knitting baskets and quilt panels onto the large table.

"Where is Thelma?" Tessa asks as she sets her sweater on her chair.

"She is in the kitchen getting the refreshments ready," Phoebe says as she sits down and starts spreading out her quilt panel.

The doorbell rings again.

"I'll get it," Bessi says on her way to the kitchen. "Well hello, Elinore and Iona. Did you ride over together?"

"Yes, we thought since we both need to go back to town before going home, then we might as well ride together," Elinore says with a smile. "And how are you dear? I heard of your weird dream from the other night. You poor thing."

"Yes, I wish I didn't have these dreams. However, they are giving everyone something to talk about," Bessi says, hugging Elinore, then Iona. "Everyone is already in the knitting room and Thelma is in the kitchen getting things ready."

"We probably will not finish the quilt today. But, I do feel up to some serious stitching," Elinore says with Iona agreeing.

"I just have several more hours on my panel and I'll be finished," Bessi says, following Iona and Elinore into the knitting room.

"We can always stitch all the panels together then work on the areas we need to finish later," Iona says, giving Tessa a hug and light kiss on the cheek. "Hello, dear."

"I agree. We could just spend today getting the quilt together. While some work on the edge pattern, others could finish their panel," Iona says with another hug and kiss to Phoebe.

"All right, everyone is here so I'll get the beverages and snacks," Thelma says, and then returns rolling a large cart into the room with a large tray on top.

"We are all ready to knit and talk," Pheobe says as she pours herself some tea and then returns to her chair where she begins to work on her panel.

"Which tea are we drinking this time?" Tessa asks as she pours herself a cup and returns to her chair.

"It's called soul soother," Thelma replies with a chuckle from everyone around the room. "Now that we are all settled down for knitting, let's hear about Bessi's last few dreams."

"Oh, do tell, Bessi," Tessa says with several of the other women agreeing.

"Well, some of you have already heard of the last few dreams so bear with me as I tell the rest of you the stories," Bessi says as she picks up her knitting tools and begins knitting on her quilt panel. "Last night, I dreamed I was sailing with someone who I think was my husband. While I was pulling in a net full of clean dishes that the fish nibbled clean, the boat came to a stop. The other person, who I'll just say was my husband, jumped overboard and swam to a small sandy beach on a very small island. The only thing on the island was a small tree at the center. Then, my husband started to gather items from the waves. They kept accumulating and accumulating until the island was covered with them. My husband then integrated with these objects and turned into some weird abstract object. The boat suddenly began to drift away and the island became a mound of foaming bubbles. Then I woke up," Bessi says, taking a drink of tea.

"Well!" Tessa says. "That would have put me in the loony bin."

"You and me both," Elinore says.

"Maybe the dream is a sign that your husband is becoming too materialistic?" Phoebe says with several giggles from around the room.

"That could be it," Bessi says. "I wish understanding my dreams were that simple."

"Well, you don't even know if the person in your dream was your husband," Iona says as she pulls as stitch through her quilt panel.

"That's right. You are only assuming that because it was a man," Thelma says, drinking her tea.

"Maybe it is a dream to explain all men?" Tessa says with another giggle from around the room.

"I wish I could be so light about the dream, and I probably should be, but these dreams really bug me," Bessi says, repositioning her quilt panel.

"They would bug any of us, dear," Thelma says with everyone agreeing. "If you don't mind talking about the dreams, could you tell us the one about the green pig?"

"Certainly," Bessi says, taking another drink of her tea. "The dream started with me hanging from a branch in a pine tree. Across from me was a green pig standing on a branch. The pig asked me to lift my ankles up to him and he would swing me out into the soft needles. I did so and the pig tells me to let go, so I do. I swing gently out into the soft needles of the pine tree, and then hear the pig giggle and he lets me go. I begin to fall through the branches and I keep falling and falling," Bessi says, continuing to rethread a different colored thread.

"That dream clearly is a warning about men," Iona says with several of the others laughing with her.

"Whatever it meant, it wasn't a good dream," Bessi says, looking around the room. "That same night, I fell back asleep and ended up in the same dream with the same green pig. I was following him through some orange sand dunes and we came across a group of tanned women in their forties all dressed in these dresses made of mirrors. The women were combing each other's hair while one of the women read from a black book. The green pig asked them something and they all laughed at him so he walked away and I followed. We then came upon a group of tanned men about the same age, also wearing mirrored body suits that showed off their genitals and muscles. These men were all reading from the same black book. The green pig asked them something and they all pointed to where the sun was beginning to set. So, the pig went that way and I followed him until we came up to a cliff that overlooked a great ocean of wrinkled light reflection. The green pig mumbled something to me and then jumped into the air, descending into the light. I looked behind me at the two groups of people approaching, all waving black books. I tried to think about what was going on, but couldn't. After several moments, I jumped into the air and began falling into the light. I woke up grasping my pillow and waking my husband," Bessi says, taking another drink of her tea.

"That one was weirder than the other one," Elinore says with a shake of her head.

"It leaves me speechless," Phoebe says while staring at Bessi.

"Again, I agree," Thelma says as she repositions her quilt panel. "Well, not to change the subject, but my panel is ready to be added to all of yours."

"Mine too," Bessi says. "I can do the last of the fine stitch work after I do the final edging."

"Well, it looks like we are all ready. So let's decide whose panel gets positioned where," Elinore says as she spreads her panel out in front of her.

"Good idea," Tessa says as she spreads her panel out in front of her.

"We can all finish spreading out our panels and then maybe place them in different sequences to see what looks the best," Phoebe says with every one agreeing.

"Since they all have a sort of fall color to them, it probably doesn't matter where any one panel goes," Bessi says as she stands up and looks down at the panels all spread out.

"I agree. They look fine just the way they are right now," Thelma says with every one agreeing.

"So then, let's begin connecting them," Iona says as she sits back down and begins putting pins along the inside edge of her panel.

"Let the pinning begin," Phoebe says as everyone sits back down and begins to pin the inside edges of their panels.

"How about another story Bessi?" Elinore asks.

"Well, there was one dream last week that I haven't told anyone about yet," Bessi says, standing back up to get more tea.

"Oh, do tell," Tessa says, lifting her cup in a gesture for a refill.

"Anyone else care for more tea?" Bessi asks as she takes the teapot around the room and fills everyone's cup.

"Well, there must be a reason that you haven't told anyone about this dream, Bessi," Thelma says.

"Yes, it was very disturbing," Bessi says as she looks around the room at everyone staring at her.

"You don't have to tell us you know," Elinore says with a gentle head gesture.

"Oh, yes she does," Iona says with a giggle. "It is very healthy for Bessi to talk about these dreams so they don't stay all bottled up inside her."

"I agree," Bessi says as she begins pinning her panel's inside edge together with Thelma's bottom inside edge.

"Before we get into another dream, Thelma, what happened with the gray gopher eating your purple iris patch?" Phoebe asks as she folds back her top inside edge.

"Oh, you'll never guess what Bessi came up with," Thelma says as she positions her panel's top inside edge next to Elinore's bottom inside edge. "Well, you all remember those stray cats that stayed in our garage when Arlo was still alive?" She says, looking around the room.

"Yes, a black cat and an orange one," Tessa says.

"Yes," Thelma says. "Anyway, Arlo used to insist that the cats always had fresh dry cat food and he would toss the uneaten food, after it sat out for three days of so, over into that area of the yard. Well, Bessi came up with the idea that the flavor of the cat food got into the iris bulbs somehow and that old gray gopher has taken a fancy to them," she says with an approving smile to Bessi.

"It was only a suggestion," Bessi says with a smile.

"What a clever deduction, Bessi," Elinore says with a smile.

"Clever indeed," Phoebe says. "I never would have come up with that."

"Either would I," Iona says with a smile.

"None of us would have," Thelma says with a smile.

"Well, what about that other dream, Bessi?" Elinore asks.

"Oh, yes. The one I didn't want to tell anyone about," Bessi says as she finishes placing the pins on all three of her inside panel edges. "I'll wait to do my stitching until we all get our pins in," she says, leaning back in her chair and sipping some more tea. "This dream was the strangest dream yet. It started out on a grassy knoll in the clouds. I was watching two angels relaxing in the grass and then they became passionate with one another. Suddenly there was thunder and great vibrations and the clouds all turned dark. A big voice said something to them and one of them flew away, head down, and the other was flung into the clouds, landing on Earth. The voice said several things to the angel and the angel turned away and started walking Earth alone. After what seemed a short time, the angel came upon a group of large human-like monkeys and he began to play with them. The angel then took one of the female monkeys and made love to her. Again, thunder filled the sky and several bolts of lightening hit the angel. The noise went away and the monkeys helped the angel. More time passed and the monkey had a baby and it looked like a human," Bessi says, shaking her head. "I wanted to wake up but couldn't. The angel, the female monkey, and the human-like baby were cast out from the other monkeys. They began to create more babies until there were naked humans of all ages running all over the place," Bessi says, looking around the room at stunned expressions.

"Bessi, that dream would haunt me if it came from my mind," Tessa says with a stunned look.

"I think I would commit myself to an insane asylum," Phoebe says with a chuckle.

"It is no wonder you are so upset by your dreams, Bessi," Iona says. "That dream would have me in church every day praying for hours on end."

"Whatever good that would do," Tessa says. "Bessi, these dreams are amazing. You should really try writing them down. You could publish a book of dreams at the rate your going," Thelma says as she pricks her finger with a needle. "Ouch!"

"I just wish I could understand why I am having all these visions and dreams in the first place," Bessi says as she hands Thelma a tissue for her finger.

"There must be a reason," Iona says as she finishes the last pin on her panel. "Have you discussed these dreams with your doctor yet?"

"I have an appointment to see him next week," Bessi says, getting up and pouring more tea for herself and everyone in the room.

"Maybe you have a brain tumor and something like that?" Tessa says with a shrug of her shoulders.

"Oh, Tessa!" Thelma says with a frown. "Bessi doesn't need to worry about something like that now. She is just probably going through a hormone imbalance or something simple like a mid-life crisis."

"What does that dream book that you borrowed from Miss Wellsby say, Bessi?" Elinore asks.

"Well, so far, it has only described the biological process in which we dream and not anything about what dreams mean or where they come from. But, I am only half-way through it, so maybe I will find out as I read more," Bessi says as she takes in a deep breath. "I am hoping it will tell me about the world we go to when we dream."

"You poor dear," Thelma says with a shake of her head. "I would love to just tell you that all these dreams are just in your head and that there is no other world except for the one we wake up in every morning."

"Wouldn't that be simple enough?" Elinore says as she begins to put her things into the knitting box.

"In reality, no one knows anything about any world outside of this one," Tessa says as she begins to put her things away.

"Heaven has always been a dream of mine," Iona says as she sips her tea.

"Well, no one knows if that even exists," Thelma says as she finishes pinning her quilt panel's last inside corner.

"Maybe when we dream we get a glimpse of what heaven is," Phoebe says as she begins to put her knitting items away in her box.

"If that was the case, I wouldn't want to be in the areas of heaven that I have been dreaming about," Bessi says as she begins to put her things away.

"Well, we will probably never know unless Bessi has some other dreams that tell us differently," Iona says as she stands and takes her cup over to the tray on the cart.

"Thelma, Iona and I will help clean up today," Elinore says as she begins to collect the cups.

"Oh, thank you. We can leave the rest of the quilting supplies out so we can finish up on Wednesday."

"We should be able to finish the quilt that day," Phoebe says as she stands up and looks at the quilt all pinned together. "It is sure going to be a great prize for the fundraiser."

"We'll have to start another one soon," Thelma says as she begins to push the cart into the kitchen.

"OK everyone, I am going. I have a few things to do," Bessi says as she hugs Tessa and then Elinore.

"You take care, dear, and don't let those dreams get the better of you," Elinore says with Tessa agreeing.

"Be sure you talk with your doctor. Maybe there is something he can do to help," Phoebe says as she gives Bessi a hug.

"Will you be dropping by the store later today dear?" Iona says as she gives Bessi a hug.

"Yes, I need to get some more of that delicious corn," Bessi says as she hugs Thelma. "Thank you for all of your support, Thelma."

"Why of course, dear. What are friends for?" Thelma asks, kissing Bessi on the cheek. "You say hello to that family of yours OK?"

"All right," Bessi says, opening the door and leaving the house. As she drives away, she glances over her shoulder and waves at her friends standing at the door waving back.

On the way home, Bessi stops to get gas at one of the local gas stations. "Hello, Mr. Otterstad, could you please check the oil too?" Bessi says, pulling the lever under her steering wheel to release the hood.

"Sure thing, Bessi," Mr. Otterstad says with a smile. "I wish you would just call me Walter," he says with a wink.

"You know my husband is jealous of you and I don't want to add to that," Bessi says with a smile.

"Well, you were supposed to marry me," Walter says as he sets the gas nozzle and then returns to the front of the car.

"I know, Walter. And, there are times I wish I had," Bessi says, smiling from inside the car.

"It's not too late you know," Walter says as he walks over to the car window and lets her see the dipstick. "It looks about a half a quart too low. I think I have an open quart in the shop. I'll get it," Walter says. "Why don't you come in and see how organized the shop is now?"

"You know I couldn't do that without everyone talking about us being together," Bessi says with a smile. "Especially when everyone knows we were school sweethearts."

"Yeah, we sure were," Walter says, stepping into the garage and then out again. "I still don't understand why you chose Mr. Hornsdecker over me?" Walter says with a smile.

"I don't know either, Walter," Bessi says, staring at him through the windshield as he puts down the hood.

"Well, like I said it's never too late, old girlfriend," Walter says with a smile.

"I have my children to think about," Bessi says. "Besides, the folks in town wouldn't go along with us being together, and you know that," she says with laughter.

"This town wouldn't mind. It will give them something to talk about," Walter says as he wipes his hands on a rag, standing by the driver's door. "And about those kids of yours, they are heading off to college soon."

"You'll never give up, will you Walter?" Bessi asks with a smile.

"You'll always be my girl, Bessi," Walter says, walking back to the gas pump.

"Even after all these years, you would still have me?" Bessi asks as she hands him a twenty-dollar bill.

"I'll wait until the day I die for you," Walter says as he takes the twenty dollars. "That will be fourteen dollars and seventy-two cents."

"Oh Walter, what will I do with you?" Bessi says with a smile as she watches him take out the change from his pocket. "I will never get over you either. If I weren't married, I would run into your arms and never let go."

"Like I said, I'll be waiting," Walter says, handing Bessi the change. "Now you better scoot before I lose my self-control and get all teary-eyed," He says, walking away.

"Bye, Walter," Bessi says, getting teary-eyed as she drives away. She looks back one last time and waves. As she drives through town, she remembers what great times she had with Walter and some of her other friends who have moved away.

Bessi decides to stop by the local nursery to pick up some plants for her garden. As she pulls up to the nursery's gate, she feels better seeing another former schoolmate William Knottsinger, the nursery owner.

"Well hello there, Bessi!" William says as he puts down the wheelbarrow full of manure.

"Well, hello to you, William," Bessi says as she gets out of her car and gives William a hug.

"How are the kids and hubby?" William says with a smile.

"There are all fine," Bessi says as she steps over to some new flower seedlings just popping up from a flat of soil. "And what do you having popping up here?"

"Miss Wellsby wanted some multi-colored straw flowers for her front yard so I planted her a few flats of them," William says as he picks up the wheelbarrow again and starts walking with Bessi as she strolls toward the larger manure pile.

"William, I would like something unique to plant in my yard," Bessi says as she looks around at the many varieties of plants.

"Well, something for color or something for eating?" William asks as he dumps the wheelbarrow out and then puts it aside.

"I wish I knew," Bessi says indecisively. "I just want something different."

"Well, I just got in these new dwarf apple trees called Wallaby's Anchor," William says as he points over to the young trees.

"Wallaby's Anchor, what kind of name is that?" Bessi asks with a smile.

"From what I gathered from the catalog, this guy Wallaby did some cross-breeding and the apples grow in the shape of a small anchor," William says with a smile. "Supposedly they are real tasty."

"And they are dwarf trees?" Bessi asks as she touches one of the trees.

"As dwarfed as they get," William says, sliding one out from the group. "I'll tell you what, you take this one for free and plant it. You'll be the first person in Soul Stead to have one," William says with a smile.

"Oh, you don't have to do that William. I'll pay you for it," Bessi says, looking at the small but healthy tree. "How much does it cost?"

"Well, if you won't let me give it to you, then you'll have to at least accept it for the price I paid for it," William says as he grabs the small tree and begins walking toward Bessi's car.

"You are too kind, William," Bessi says as she follows him back to her car, opening the passenger door and rolling down the window. "So, how much do I owe you for this rare apple tree?"

"Twelve dollars," William says as he places the tree at the foot of the passenger seat and then closes the door with the top of the tree partially hanging out of the window.

"Can I just give you a twenty and we call it even?" Bessi asks as she reaches into the driver's door window and gets her purse.

"No. Now, darn it, the cost is twelve dollars or no deal," William says with a smile.

"All right then let me see if I have exact change," Bessi says as she looks in her wallet and brings out a ten-dollar bill and two one-dollar bills. "There. You run a hard bargain, Mr. Knottsinger," She says with a smile.

"Now don't over water it," William says as Bessi gets into her car. "In the catalog it said that one of its distant relatives was from a drought-resistant family," William says with a smile as he puts the cash in his front pocket. He waves to Bessi when she smiles and drives away with the small tree partially hanging out of her car window.

Bessi stops by the grocery store and tells Iona about her new tree while picking up a few things for dinner, including the corn. She then makes her way home and, after a brief nap, she begins to dig the hole for her new tree.

"Hello there, Bessi," her neighbor, Mrs. Brooks, says. "What you planting there?"

"Oh hello, Mrs. Brooks," Bessi says, continuing to dig her hole. "It is a dwarf apple tree I picked up from Mr. Knottsinger's Nursery."

"Oh my, how neat," Mrs. Brooks says as she waves to Bessi. "I'll look forward to being one of the first people to try one of those apples."

"OK, Mrs. Brooks. It will be next year some time," Bessi says, shaking her head as she watches Mrs. Brooks get into her car and drive off.

Suddenly from the front of the house, Silus starts calling out, "Bessi, Bessi."

"I am in the back yard, dear," Bessi says as she puts down the shovel and goes into the house.

"There you are," Silus says as he looks very upset. "Do you know what they are saying all over town right now?"

"No, what, dear? What is wrong?" Bessi asks as she thinks about Walter Otterstad.

"People are talking about your dreams all over town. Someone actually came into the church and said that you had a dream about mankind being from a devil-raping a monkey," Silus says as he hits his forehead with his hand. "I don't believe this."

"Honey, I did have a dream about that but I just told a few people in my quilting group about it," Bessi says as she sits down on a kitchen stool.

"This dream stuff has to stop. You are to not tell any one about your ridiculous dreams, do you hear me?" Silus asks. "I just hope the kids don't get teased at school," he says, getting a glass from the cupboard and filling it with water.

"I will tell anyone I want to tell about my dreams, including our children," Bessi says as she stands up and walks over to the sink.

"Why? Why do you have to drag everyone else into your insanity? Are we all to suffer because you can't get a grip on your dreams?" Silus asks as he sets the glass on the counter. "Do you know what they are saying at the church? They think you are crazy. They want to know if you really dreamed that horrible concept or are just going mad."

"It was only a dream," Bessi says as she leans against the counter.

"Well, your dream might have just caused me a bunch of trouble. You're a preacher's wife, and as my wife, you don't go around spreading stories like that," Silus says as he throws his hands into the air.

"I am sorry. I just thought I would tell a few of my friends about the dream. That's all," Bessi says as she folds her arms and looks out the kitchen window at her new tree.

"Honey, just think next time before you tell anyone about your dreams. By now, it has probably reached the Vatican," Silus says as he leaves the kitchen and then exits the house to drive back to the church.

Bessi finishes his glass of water and returns to planting her dwarf apple tree. A little while later, as she finishes planting the tree, Louisa approaches.

"Mom, are you all right?" she asks.

"Yes, of course dear. Why do you ask?" Bessi replies.

"I saw Dad and he seemed pretty upset about something that you dreamed," Louisa says as she hugs her mother.

"Oh, it will be all right. Your father is just overreacting," Bessi says as she picks up the shovel and watering jug.

"What kind of tree is this, Mom?" Louisa asks her mother as she touches one of the tree's leaves.

"It is a new kind of dwarf apple tree that I got from Mr. Knottsinger," Bessi says as she walks toward the house. "It is called a Wallaby's Anchor."

"That's a weird name for an apple tree, isn't it?" Louisa asks as she helps her mother put the shovel away in the garage.

"Weird indeed," Bessi says as she closes the garage door and enters the kitchen to wash her hands.

"So, this dream, about the monkey and the devil, did you really dream that, Mom?" Louisa asks with a smile as she sits on one of the kitchen stools.

"Where did you hear that?" Bessi asks with a smile.

"It is all over school. Everyone is talking about it and even several of the seniors want to do the school play about it," Louisa says with as smile.

"Oh, God."" Bessi says, drying her hands on a paper towel. "Your father would have a fit if your senior class chose to do that as their school play."

"What would you think, Mom?" Louisa asks as she turns to see Lewis come into the kitchen.

"Hello, Mom," Lewis says, giving Bessi a kiss on the cheek. "I heard about your dream. It is totally cool," Lewis says, going to the refrigerator and getting out the milk jug. "The kids at school want to know if you would let them use the story for the school play," he says, pouring milk into a glass and then returning the jug to the refrigerator.

"I wouldn't mind, but your father is having a fit over it," Bessi says as she smiles. "It was only a dream. Why does he have to get so bent out of shape over it?"

"It upsets people in the church. That's why," Lewis says with a smile.

"Well, we will have to be sympathetic to your father when he gets home. Don't give him a hard time about getting so upset over it, OK," Bessi says with a smile.

"Well, tomorrow the students will vote on if we should do our school play about it," Lewis says as he begins to leave the kitchen. "I'll be in my room doing my homework, Mom."

"All right, dear. I'll call you when supper is ready," Bessi says with a smile to Louisa who sits staring at her. "What?"

"You're cool, Mom," Louisa says as she gets up and hugs Bessi. "I'll go get my homework out of the way, too. See you at dinner, and oh, Mom, cool tree."

"Thank you, dear. See you at dinner," Bessi says as she turns to look out the kitchen window again at her dwarf apple tree.

Then the phone rings and it is Silus.

"Hello Bessi. I'll be late for dinner tonight due to conflicts brought about by the rumors of your dream. So, go ahead, you and the children eat with out me," Silus says.

"OK,dear. I am sorry this whole thing has gotten out of hand," Bessi says.

"I am too. Let's just hope that everything blows over and nothing comes of this," Silus says. "See you later, dear."

"See you later," Bessi says as she hangs up the phone. She then goes upstairs and knocks on Louisa's door. "Louisa, can I come in?"

"Sure, Mom," Louisa says from her desk while doing her homework.

"Your father just called and said he won't be here for dinner due to issues around the rumors of my dream. So, I was wondering if you could hold off on telling your father about the other students wanting to do their school play about the devil and monkey concept," Bessi says from the doorway.

"Sure, Mom," Louisa says with a smile as she watches her mother close the door.

"Lewis?" Bessi says as she knocks on his door.

"Yeah, Mom?" Lewis says from within his room.

"Can I come in?' Bessi asks.

"Sure," Lewis says as he opens the door.

"Your father just called and won't be joining us for dinner. I also wanted to ask you if you could please hold off on mentioning to him about the other students wanting to do the school play about my dream," Bessi says with a smile.

"Sure, Mom, no problem," Lewis says with a smile. "I hope we get to do the dream as our school play. It would be cool."

"Your father might have something to say about that," Bessi says with a smile. "We'll have to see how things are after he calms down. I'll call you when supper is ready," she says, closing Lewis' bedroom door and returning to the kitchen where she begins calling all of her friends who were at the quilting club that day.

"Hello, Elinore. I just talked to Thelma and she said she thought that you had mentioned my monkey dream to Mrs. Ringsfield," Bessi says.

"Well, yes I did. Was I not supposed to say anything?" Elinore asks.

"Oh, it's all right. It's just all over town now and has caused some problems at the church. That's all," Bessi says with a chuckle.

"Oh dear, I am sorry that Mrs. Ringsfield couldn't keep her yap shut," Elinore says with a chuckle.

"That is all right. I just wanted to know how it got all over town so suddenly," Bessi says as she opens up the refrigerator.

"I am sorry, dear, but with dreams like that, people want to talk about them," Elinore says.

"I guess so," Bessi says, pulling out several things and placing them on the countertop.

"What are you fixing for dinner tonight?" Elinore asks.

"Well, besides corn on the cob, I thought I would do crab cakes on red rice," Bessi says. "And you?"

"I wish I was doing something that interesting, but I am not. I decided to reheat some clam chowder from the other day," Elinore says. "Being a widow is hard on the menu."

"Well, I better get off the phone so I can start the crab cakes. Thank you for telling me about Mrs. Ringsfield."

"Oh, you're welcome, dear. I am just sorry that her gossip came from me," Elinore says as she chuckles. "Bye, dear."

"Goodbye," Bessi says as she hangs up the phone.

"Mom?" Louisa says as she enters into the kitchen. "Mrs. Barnsworth just sent me an e-mail and said she would like to talk to you about your devil-monkey dream," She says as she swipes a bite of crab cake mix from the bowl.

"Why would she want to talk to me about the dream?" Bessi says as she makes another crab cake and puts onto a plate.

"Well, it seems that all the students want your dream to be the school play, so she needs to ask for your permission. She would like to know more about the dream," Louisa says as she rinses her finger off.

"Well, I don't see any reason why I couldn't talk to her about the dream," Bessi says as she makes another crab cake. "Go ahead and e-mail her back that I would be happy to meet with her tomorrow."

"OK, Mom," Louisa says leaving the kitchen.

Bessi continues to set the table and finish preparing dinner while contemplating how she is going to deal with Silus when he gets home.

"Mom, is there anything I can do to help get dinner ready?" Lewis asks as he enters the room.

"Yes, dear. You can put the glasses on the table and could you please go tell your sister that dinner will be ready in a few minutes?"

"OK, Mom," Lewis says, setting the glasses on the table then leaving to deliver her message to Louisa.

The phone rings again and Bessi answers. "Hello."

"Hello, Bessi. This is Mrs. Barnsworth, Lewis and Louisa's drama teacher," A voice says from the other end of the phone.

"Oh yes, hello," Bessi says.

"I have heard about the dream you had and would like very much to talk to you about it," Mrs. Barnsworth says.

"All right," Bessi says.

"Our senior class wants to do a special play and they all feel strongly that your dream will be just right," Mrs. Barnsworth says.

"Well, that is perfectly all right with me," Bessi says, taking several of the cooked crab cakes from the oven onto a plate.

"Well then, could we meet tomorrow around lunch time?" Mrs. Barnsworth asks.

"That would be all right with me," Bessi says, placing the last of the crab cakes on the platter.

"All right then, how about around noon at the public library?" Mrs. Barnsworth says.

"Great, I'll see you then. Bye," Bessi says.

"Thank you and good bye," Mrs. Barnsworth says.

"Mom, was that Mrs. Barnsworth?" Louisa asks as she enters into the kitchen.

"Yes, dear, we are going to meet at the library during lunch and discuss the dream," Bessi says as she places the crab cakes and corn on the cob on the table.

Lewis enters the room. "Who was that on the phone Mom?" he asks, sitting at the table.

"It was your teacher, Mrs. Barnsworth," Bessi says, sitting down at the table.

"She wants to meet Mom tomorrow at the library to discuss her dream," Louisa says as she sits at the table and starts dishing up her crab cakes.

"Cool, I hope we get to do the dream for our school play," Lewis says, putting food on his plate.

"Well, let's hope your father doesn't have a big reaction to the idea," Bessi says, dishing up a plate for Silus and then taking it into the kitchen where she places it in the oven to keep warm.

"Why is dad having such a fit about the dream anyway?" Lewis asks as he takes a bite of crab cake.

"Well, it seems that it threatens the church somehow and makes people uneasy," Bessi says as she takes a bite of her crab cake.

"It just seems that people should accept it as a dream and leave it at that," Louisa says as she begins to eat.

"Well, that sounds simple enough doesn't it?" Bessi says.

"It is going to make a cool play. I hope I get to play the devil," Lewis says, taking another bite of crab cake.

"Oh, I hope not. Your father would not like that at all," Bessi says.

"It is just a play, Mom," Lewis says.

"That is just not a part for a preacher's son to play," Bessi says with a smile.

"Hello, hello. Sorry that I am late," Silus says as he enters the room.

"I'll get your plate, dear. It is in the oven keeping warm," Bessi says as she gets up and goes into the kitchen. Upon returning, she places the dish on the table in front of Silus.

"Well, did everyone have a good day?" Silus asks as he takes a bite of crab cake.

"Yes, I did," Lewis says.

"Yes, me too," Louisa says as she takes another bite of crab cake.

"And you, dear?" Silus asks.

"Oh, I planted a fruit tree in the back yard," Bessi says as she takes a drink of water.

"Another fruit tree. What is it this time?" Silus asks.

"It's a dwarf apple tree. One of the first of its kind planted in our town, according to Mr. Knottsinger."

"I thought we already had an apple tree. What do we need with another one?" Mr. Hornsdecker asks, taking another bite.

"I just thought it wouldn't hurt to have another apple tree. Anyway, we use all the apples every year during the church's apple bake-off every fall," Bessi says, looking over at the kids.

"I guess you're right. One can't have too many apples," Silus says as he takes a drink of water. "Any peculiar things going on at school kids?"

"What do you mean dad?" Lewis asks.

"I mean, did you hear any weird rumors or stories going around campus?" Silus asks while looking over at Bessi.

"Well, just the rumors about Mom's dream being this year's senior play," Louisa says.

"What? Mrs. Barnsworth wants the seniors to turn your dream into their school play?" Silus asks, as he sets down his fork.

"Well, she is just going with what the students want to do. They want to do something different this year," Bessi says, looking across the table at Louisa.

"Yeah Dad, the dream would make a great play," Lewis says.

"I can't believe what I am hearing," Silus says as he gets up from the table. "I am going to call Sheriff Barnsworth and ask him to talk to his wife . We'll put a stop to this right now," he says, leaving the room.

"Why is Dad so opposed to the dream, Mom?" Lewis asks.

"I don't know, dear, but I think it might be because of pressure from the church," Bessi says.

"Probably a bunch of those old nags down there are complaining to him about the dream," Louisa says as she takes another bite of crab cake.

"Louisa!" Bessi says, "It's not nice to say things like that."

"Well, it is true. Those old women sit down there and dictate what they want Dad to do with the church," Louisa says, taking a drink of water.

"Louisa, I am shocked that you think your father is dictated by those kinds of people," Bessi says as she takes a drink of water.

"Why else would Dad be so against the school using the dream as a play?" Lewis asks.

"Well, he probably has his reasons," Bessi says, seeing Silus come back in the room.

"Sheriff Barnsworth says it is out of his control," Silus says as he sits down at the table. "And, as for you wanting to know my reasons for being against the dream as a school play," he pauses taking a drink of water. "I think the dream's meaning demoralizes our religion and gives people an idea that does not nurture religion. Instead, it discredits religion to a point where people are influenced not to believe and have faith."

"Honey, people who truly believe in Christianity are not going to budge from their faith because of some idea that comes from some dream," Bessi says, looking over at her husband.

"Those are not the people I am referring to, dear. I am referring to the people that are on the edge of faith and are easily influenced by ideas like that dream," Silus says as he takes another bite of his crab cake.

"But it is just a dream, Dad," Louisa says as she finishes the last bite of her dinner.

"Yes, and it should stay that way," Silus says as he finishes his dinner.

"Well, I for one still hope that the dream can be made into our school play," Lewis says as he finishes his dinner.

"We will see about that, young man," Silus says as he gets up from the table. "That was a great dinner, Bessi," he says leaving the room for his home office.

"What do you think Dad is going to do, Mom?" Louisa says as she begins to stack the dinner plates.

"I don't know, dear. He may speak to the school principal or even speak to some of the other seniors' parents to try and persuade them not to do the play," Bessi says as she carries several of the drinking glasses into the kitchen.

"Dad will just have to get over it," Lewis says as he carries in the silverware from the dinner table. "I mean, the church can't control freedom of speech,"

"I agree, Lewis," Bessi says as she begins to rinse the dishes.

"I'll wash," Lewis says.

"I'll rinse," Louisa says.

"Well, then I'll dry and put them away," Bessi says as she begins to wipe down the countertop.

"I understand Dad's point about people who are easily persuaded and that they should be protected from ideas that could harm them," Lewis says. "But, on the other hand, maybe other concepts will open their minds, help them to grow and learn to make their own choice about their religious beliefs."

"And even come up with a belief of their own," Louisa says as she begins rinsing the dishes that Lewis has washed.

"Maybe this dream will actually have a positive influence on people. Maybe they will be inspired to think about religion and come to an understanding of what they may want to believe," Lewis says, washing another plate.

"That is a good point, dear," Bessi says as she puts the silverware in the drawer after she dries them off.

"Who is to say what inspiration may come to someone that sees the play and becomes more religious in their own way," Lewis says as he finishes the last of the dishes.

"I agree with you and I am sure once things settle down, that your father will see that this idea may have some benefit to it," Bessi says. "If anything, it will get people to talk about religion."

"And, the more people talking about religion, the more likely they are to become religiously conscious, in one way or another," Louisa says as she sees her father enter the kitchen.

"Well, I see you three have figured out all aspects of this ordeal," Silus says as he leans against the counter and folds his arms across his chest.

"We were just trying to point out some positive aspects of the situation, dear," Bessi says.

"I overheard some of them. And, yes, controversy can have a positive influence as well as a negative one. Let's just hope that there is a more positive impact over this," Silus says as he leans forward. "Well, I am heading off to bed. It has been a stressful day and I am tired."

"Good night, Daddy," Louisa says, giving her father a hug.

"Good night, Dad," Lewis says, hugging his father.

"I'll be up shortly, dear," Bessi says as she kisses Silus on the cheek. "Thank you for showing some understanding in this situation."

"I am trying to keep an open mind through all this," Silus says as he leaves the kitchen and then heads up the stairs to his bedroom.

"Good night, Mom," Louisa says as she gives her mother a kiss on the cheek and goes to her room.

"Good night, Mom," Lewis says as he leaves the room to go to bed.

Bessi finishes some kitchen duties and then turns off the lights before going upstairs to her bedroom. After changing into her nightgown, she nestles into her side of the bed and begins to read her dream book. After about half an hour, she stops reading and turns off her light before nestling under her covers to sleep.

About two in the morning, Bessi wakes up from another strange dream. She quietly gets out of bed and takes her dream book downstairs. After getting a glass of water, she gets a notepad from the kitchen drawer and sits in the living room to write down her dream.

"Mom, are you all right?" Louisa asks as she enters into the living room.

"Oh, did I wake you up?" Bessi says, setting down her notepad.

"No, I was already awake and I heard you in the kitchen," Louisa says as she kneels down next to her mother in front of the chair.

"I had a weird dream so I decided to come downstairs and write the dream down," Bessi says, looking at the notepad with just a few lines written on it.

"What was your dream, Mom?" Louisa asks.

"Well, it had aliens in it and they were flying people off to somewhere," Bessi says with a smirk.

"Was it a scary dream?" Louisa asks.

"No, it's just the spaceship was taking other people away to some place safe and leaving me behind because I didn't have enough compassion for the world," Bessi says, tapping the pen on the notepad.

"You have lots of compassion, Mom," Louisa says as she rubs her mother's knee.

"Well, in the dream, I didn't do enough to save the world so they were leaving me behind. The world was going to be devastated by some weird explosion. I saw the explosion coming at me and then I woke up," Bessi says as she takes a deep breath.

"If anyone was going to be saved, it would be you, Mother. God is not going to leave you behind because you didn't save the world," Louisa says. "If that were the case, no one would be leaving the planet and we would all be destroyed,"

"I guess you're right and besides, it was just a dream," Bessi says, running her hand down Louisa's hair. "Why don't you go on up to bed and get some sleep?"

"OK, Mom," Louisa says as she stands and kisses her mother on the cheek. "Good night."

"Good night, dear," Bessi says as she picks up the pad and begins to read what she had written. She then begins writing again. Several pages later, Bessi decides to go back to bed to try and sleep.

The alarm clock goes off at six thirty in the morning. Bessi did not completely fall asleep, but did get more rest. Her husband gets out of bed first and begins his day by showering. Bessi gets up and goes downstairs and starts fixing breakfast.

"Good morning, Mom," Lewis says, standing in front of the refrigerator holding a glass half full of juice.

"Good morning, dear," Bessi says as she kisses him on the cheek and pats him on the head.

"How did you sleep last night, Mom?" Lewis asks as he drinks the last of the juice.

"Not as well as I would have liked," Bessi says as she fills the coffeepot with water.

"What did you dream about?" Lewis says as he rinses the glass and sets it on the side of the sink.

"Oh, let me tell you after school. I don't want it influencing your school day," Bessi says with a smile. "Actually, when you get home I'll let you read the dream from my new journal."

"You started a dream journal?" Lewis asks.

"Well, I am starting to write out my dreams starting with the dream from last night," Bessi says as she puts water for oatmeal on the stove to heat.

"I can't wait to read it. I hope you write down the devil's monkey dream as well," Lewis says as he walks over to the door of the kitchen to leave.

"I think that today I'll write out that dream so Mrs. Barnsworth will have it to read for our discussion," Bessi says with a yawn.

"Cool, Mom. I'll go and get ready for school," Lewis says, exiting the kitchen and heading upstairs to his room.

"Why is Lewis so excited?" Silus asks as he enters into the kitchen and pours a cup of coffee.

"I told him I was starting a dream journal today and I would let him read it after school," Bessi says as she pours herself a cup of coffee.

"I wish you would think first before you tell anyone about some of your dreams," Silus says as he goes to retrieve the newspaper from the front yard.

"Good morning, Mom," Louisa says as she enters the kitchen. "This morning, I can't stay for breakfast. A few of the girls are going to school early to beat the guys to the track," Louisa says as she kisses her mother on the cheek.

"I wish you and your peers would stop this competitive behavior with the boys," Bessi says with a smile.

"It's not competitive behavior. It is more like we're forcing the evolution of equality," Louisa says as she turns to see her father enter into the kitchen.

"What's this about equality?" Silus says as he kisses Louisa on the cheek and sits down at the dining table to read the paper.

"Mom thinks that our trying to take over the running track from the boys is competitive behavior. I was saying that I thought it was more like we were forcing the evolution of equality. The boys think that they can dominate the running track and the girls are going to show them that we are just as fast as they are," Louisa says as she sits next to her father at the table.

"Well it sounds like male-female competition to me too," Silus says with a smile as he turns another page of the newspaper.

"Oh, you're not even listening, Dad. I'll see you both after school," Louisa says as she exits the kitchen through the back door.

"Was that Louisa sneaking out the back door?" Lewis asks as he enters the kitchen.

"Yes and I wish you two would stop this competitive behavior and start eating breakfast again," Bessi says as she stirs oatmeal into the boiling water.

"Not until the girls realize that boys are designed to run faster. We are faster," Lewis says as he opens the back door.

"Well, evolution has proven that women are just as fast as men," Silus says as he turns another page of the newspaper.

"And are equal," Bessi adds as she places the lid on the oatmeal and turns the heat down low.

"Not at our school," Lewis says, closing the door as he runs off.

"You're at least staying to eat breakfast, right?" Bessi asks as she sits down at the table and picks up the front page of the newspaper.

"Yes, dear, I am staying for breakfast. Honey, I wanted to talk to you too. I think your dreams are really troubling you and I think maybe you should make an appointment with a psychiatrist," Silus says, setting the newspaper down.

"I have thought about that," Bessi says as she gets up to turn off the stove and begins dishing up the oatmeal. "And, I don't think I would have any problem with doing that, if you don't."

"Good, then today call Dr. Sackert and ask for a referral to a Dr. Effenhart. He has a private practice in town and he knows something about dreams. I have already spoken to him about our situation and he said he would be willing to help you," Silus says as he begins eating his oatmeal.

"All right, I'll try and set up an appointment for this week," Bessi says as she begins to eat her oatmeal.

"Great, and If I could add one more thing?" Silus asks. "Would you please keep some of your dreams private? This devil's monkey dream has caused me plenty of trouble at the church and as you know, there is enough scandal going on in religion with all this child molestation within the Christian church."

"Yes, I'll refrain from sharing any more of my dreams that seem detrimental to the Church of Christ," Bessi says with a light smile.

"It's not just that some of your dreams are detrimental to our church. Your dreams could influence other people's grasp on reality," Silus says as he takes another bite of his oatmeal.

"Almost everything anyone experiences in life influences their grasp of reality," Bessi says as she takes a sip of coffee.

"Well, in this case, you have control of how you influence people and you should take that responsibly," Silus says as he starts folding the newspaper.

"I see your point and it is well taken. However, a lot of people don't share your views about this dream with the devil and the monkey. The students have their minds set on this dream being their school play and I don't see any reason why they can't do it," Bessi says, taking their bowls into the kitchen.

"What has gotten into you?" Silus asks. "I am going to see what I can do to stop that play. In the mean time, you pursue some therapy and try and see things from a sensible point of view," he says, getting up from the table.

"Let's not get bent out of shape over this," Bessi says, going up to Silus and giving him a kiss on the cheek.

"I'm not getting bent out of shape. I am just making a stand about how I feel about the situation," Silus says as he grabs the newspaper and begins to leave the kitchen. "I'll finish the paper at the church."

"OK, dear," Bessi says, pouring herself another cup of coffee. Hearing the front door close, she releases a big sigh. She then cleans up the kitchen and returns to the bedroom where she lies down on the bed to take a fresh look at things.

After about a half-hour, Bessi sits up and begins reading her dream book. She then realizes that today she needs to stop by the library to let Miss Wellsby know she is making progress with the book and that she will return it to her by the end of next week.

As she reads, she comes across some paragraphs that reveal something about spirituality. The book suggests that the spirit co-exists in a parallel realm and evolves as we live through each day. She sets down the book and begins to let the idea run freely through her mind. She then begins to get insight about her own spiritual development and the possible truth of there being another realm.

Several hours pass and Bessi wakes because the ringing phone near her bed. "Hello, hello," she says as she answers the phone.

"Hello, Bessi. Are you all right dear?" Thelma asks.

"Oh hello, Thelma. Yes, I'm all right. I've just been napping, that's all," Bessi says as she sits up in bed.

"You poor dear. Are those crazy dreams still bothering you?" Thelma asks.

"I've had a few since we last spoke. I just woke up from one that I wouldn't have minded staying in," she says with a smile.

"Well, I didn't mean to interrupt a pleasant dream, but I was wondering if you would have time to stop by and help with a few bulbs in my garden today," Thelma asks.

"Why certainly. What time?" Bessi asks.

"Any time this afternoon would be right for me. I have a hair appointment this morning at ten o'clock," Thelma says.

"What time is it? Oh dear, it's already a quarter past nine," Bessi says as she rubs the top of her head. "I can't believe I slept for over an hour."

"You must have been tired dear. OK, so I'll see you some time mid-day then?" Thelma asks.

"All right, I'll see you then," Bessi says hanging up the phone. She then gets up and goes into the bathroom to prepare herself for the day.

After showering, dressing, and putting on her makeup, she then makes the bed and tidies up the house before she leaves for her daily errands.

As Bessi enters town, her first stop is the library where she meets one of the congregation in the parking lot.

"Hello, Bessi," Mrs. Brooks says as she unlocks her car door.

"Oh hello, Mrs. Brooks. How are you doing?" Bessi asks, walking past the front of the vehicle. "How is the family?"

"Fine, fine. Sharon told me about their senior class wanting to do that devil and monkey dream of yours as their school play," Mrs. Brooks says as she steps toward the front of her vehicle.

"Yes, I heard about that too," Bessi says as she stops in front of the car next to Mrs. Brooks. "I guess the whole town has heard about that silly dream by now."

"Oh, I am sure of that," Mrs. Brooks says with a light laugh and a gesture with her hands. "As weird as that story is, everyone is talking about it."

"Unfortunately, there is some controversy over it," Bessi says with a shrug of her shoulders.

"Well, you have to admit that it is a very strange concept and does tend to be rather disturbing," Mrs. Brooks says with a facial expression.

"I guess so," Bessi says as she begins to step away. "I need to get into the library. So I'll be seeing you at church on Sunday?"

"You take care, dear, and we'll see you Sunday," Mrs. Brooks says as she turns to open her car door.

Bessi enters the library and greets Mr. Thomas who is taping up a bulletin on one of the library windows near the front door. "Hello Mr. Thomas, could you tell me where I could find Miss Wellsby?" Bessi asks with a smile.

"Good morning to you, Mrs. Hornsdecker. Miss Wellsby is in the back room unpacking some recent deliveries," Mr. Thomas says with a smile.

"Thank you," Bessi says as she turns to walk toward the back of the library.

"Hello, Bessi," Mrs. Landis says from the end of a bookcase.

"Oh hello, Mrs. Landis," Bessi says, stopping and stepping over to the bookshelf. "How is Carol doing with her college application to Yale?"

"She is still waiting to hear back from them. By the way, I got a call from your husband this morning asking me to speak to Carol about not supporting the idea of doing that crazy dream about the devil for their senior play," Mrs. Landis says quietly.

"He did?" Bessi says with a tilt of her head.

"Yes. I told him I would have nothing to do with her decision and that it was totally up to her and her classmates," Mrs. Landis says.

"Good for you," Bessi says with a nod of her head. "I think Silus is overreacting and should not be making such a big deal out of this."

"I agree," Mrs. Landis says as she begins to walk over to Bessi. "I think he has been getting a lot of flack from some of the other church members over your dream."

"He said he had some problems at the church over this but did not go into any detail," Bessi says as she leans over to one side. "Oh, there goes Miss Wellsby. I need to speak with her for a minute. I'll see you at church on Sunday, OK?"

"I need to get going too. I'll see you Sunday," Mrs. Landis says as she begins to walk over to the checkout desk where Mr. Thomas stands sorting books.

"Hello, Miss Wellsby," Bessi says quietly.

"Oh hello, Mrs. Hornsdecker," Miss Wellsby says as she sets down a small stack of magazines on a table in the reading area.

"I just wanted to stop by and say that I am half-way through that book. It will be at least another week before I am finished with it," Bessi says with a quiet voice.

"That will be fine. There is no rush," Miss Wellsby says. "Mr. Hornsdecker was in here first thing this morning checking out a bunch of short story books. He asked about a book on traditional plays. Could you tell him that I found a book in our drama section and if he wants it, I'll keep it at the front desk for a few days?"

"Oh, OK. I didn't know he stopped by and was checking out books. He must want to give the seniors some alternative ideas for their play," Bessi says with a smile.

"I don't think he realizes that they already made up their minds about doing the devil's monkey play. Now they are arguing over who gets to play the devil and who gets to play the main monkey," Miss Wellsby says with a light chuckle.

"Oh my," Bessi says. "He is going to be really surprised to find out that his son wants to play the devil in the play."

"That would be ironic for a preacher's son to play the devil," Miss Wellsby says with a light laugh.

"I'm not sure if ironic is the word that comes to my mind," Bessi says with a worried look on her face.

"Oh, it can't be all that serious," Miss Wellsby says.

"Oh and worse," Bessi says. "Well, I better get going. I'll tell Silus about the book being at the front desk," Bessi says as she begins to walk away.

"Good luck," Miss Wellsby says with a smile.

"Thank you," Bessi says as she walks to the front of the library.

"Have a nice day, Mrs. Hornsdecker," Mr. Thomas says with a smile as he sorts through small piles of books at the front desk.

"You too, Mr. Thomas," Bessi says as she exits the library. After waving to several people, Bessi gets into her car and drives through town to the fabric store. As she parks the car, someone honks and waves at her. Bessi waves and then gets out of the car.

"Hello Molly," She says, entering the fabric store.

"Oh hello, Bessi. How are you?" Molly says from behind a pile of fabric bolts.

"I'm fine today. How are you?" Bessi asks as she runs her fingers across some silky fabric.

"Another day in the world of fabric," Molly says with a smile. "What kind of material were you looking to buy today?"

"I would like to look at some floral patterns," Bessi says as she continues to touch fabric with her hands. "I'm in the mood for something light, but heavy enough to wear into the fall season."

"All right, under that cutting table are several bolts you can look at while I round up a few more bolts," she says guiding Bessi to the other side of the room. "Is this going to be for you or something for Louisa?" Molly says as she begins to pull out floral pattern fabric bolts and lay them on the table.

"Actually, I am thinking of making us both a short dress for the rest of summer," Bessi says as she bends down next to the table and begins to feel several different fabrics. She then pulls out one of the bolts and walks over to the table where Molly is laying out several other bolts. "I kind of like this texture if you had it in a lighter color."

"I think I might have that pattern with a pinkish background," Molly says as she steps between several fabric bolt islands that are scattered through out the store.

"I think this one here with the antique white background will be fine for Louisa. She'll like the yellow roses," Bessi says as she runs her fingers across the fabric. "It has a nice feel to it and it should soften up nicely after it has been washed."

"Which one? Oh yes, that one does soften up to a nicely after washing," Molly says as she places several bolts of fabric on top of the others. "How do you like this one?" she asks as she unrolls a light colored fabric from its bolt.

"Oh, that is nice," Bessi says as she runs her fingers across the fabric. "I like it and I think that will be fine for what I have in mind."

"Great. Can you grab that rose pattern and follow me over to the cutting table?" Molly says with a smile.

"I think I need about four and a half yards of the rose pattern and about six yards of the wildflower you have there," Bessi says as she follows Molly through the maze of fabric islands over to the large cutting table.

"Which pattern are you going to use for your dress?" Molly asks as she begins to unroll the fabric.

"I thought I could use the top pattern pieces of that blouse I made last year for the town picnic," Bessi says as she looks at other fabric bolts around her.

"The one with the three-quarter length sleeves?" Molly asks as she begins to cut the fabric.

"Yes, and I thought that it and the lower part of the pattern you used for *Romeo and Juliet* would look good together," Bessi says as she takes the folded up rose pattern material from Molly.

"Oh, that is going to look great, especially with the wildflower fabric. You do have a good eye for pattern design," Molly says as she begins to unroll the wild flower fabric. "Which pattern are you going to use for Louisa's dress?"

"I haven't discussed it with Louisa yet, but I'm thinking that since she likes the shorter mid-length look, I'll use the same bottom pattern as mine and just modify it," Bessi says as she follows Molly to the front of the store. "And, since she likes to wear short sleeves, I'll use that design from the production of *Peter Pan* as the upper pattern."

"Oh, that is going to be cute," Molly says as she places the fabrics in a plastic bag. "That pattern was adorable."

"Yes, it was," Bessi says as she begins to pull out some money from her purse.

"Both fabrics were the same price at seven dollars a yard. Are you going to need to get any thread to match?" Molly asks with a smile.

"No, I think I have plenty of colors to choose from at home, but if I do, I'll be back," Bessi says with a smile.

"OK, then it comes up to seventy-nine dollars and fifty-two cents," Molly says as she takes four twenties from Bessi.

"Thank you, Molly," Bessi says as she looks around the room at the different fabric colors.

"Are you already thinking about the patterns for this year's senior play costumes?" Molly says as she hands Bessi her change.

"Yes, I'm afraid I am," Bessi says with a smile.

"Well, it won't be too hard to make a devil outfit and a bunch of monkey suits," Molly says with some laughter.

"Yes, I guess so. Do you think we'll find a monkey suit in the Halloween costume catalog?" Bessi asks as she puts her change in her purse.

"I'll see what I can come up with," Molly says with a smile. "I hear Mr. Hornsdecker is making a fuss over the students wanting to even turn the dream into a play."

"Yes, he is and we'll all have to wait to see if he is going to have any impact on their decision," Bessi says as she picks up her purchase. "Thank you again, Molly."

"You're welcome, Bessi. Say hello to Louisa for me," Molly says as she steps from behind the counter over to the table piled with fabric bolts.

"I will," Bessi says as she exits the store. Bessi glances at her watch and realizes it is nearly noon, so she heads over to the school to meet with Mrs. Barnsworth about the play.

As Bessi arrives at the school, she sees her husband's car pulling away. She tries to wave at him, but he is too preoccupied to look her way. After parking, she goes into the main entrance and runs into Mrs. Barnsworth in the hall. "Hello, Mrs. Barnsworth."

"Oh hello, Mrs. Hornsdecker. I was just talking with your husband," Mrs. Barnsworth says as she shakes Bessi's hand.

"Yes, I just saw him drive away," Bessi says with a confused expression on her face.

"Yes, well, he was here talking to the principal about the play. I don't think he was very happy when he left," Mrs. Barnsworth says as she turns and begins walking with Bessi.

"I hope he didn't cause any trouble for you," Bessi says sincerely.

"No, I can fend for myself and the principal basically told him it was out of her hands," Mrs. Barnsworth says as she moves to the side of the hall to let several students pass. "We can go up to my office to have our discussion if you would like, or we could go out and sit on the bleachers. Which would you prefer?"

"Oh, let's sit outside. It's such a nice day," Bessi says with a smile.

"Great, let's go around from the front of the school," Mrs. Barnsworth says as she turns around and begins walking in the opposite direction.

"So, are you going to let the students do the devil and monkey dream as their play?" Bessi asks as she walks along.

"I have always let the students pick their own plays, Mrs. Hornsdecker, and I am not going to change that policy now. The all know that it is going to be more work taking the dream and making it into a play, rather than just picking out a play that has already been written," Mrs. Barnsworth says.

"It's funny, but Lewis wants to play the devil in the play," Bessi says with a sigh.

"All the boys do. They agreed to pick straws to see who plays the part. The girls have decided to do the same regarding the monkey part," Mrs. Barnsworth says as she steps outside into the sunlight.

"To make it even worse, Louisa wants to play the monkey," Bessi says with a light chuckle.

"You don't think Mr. Hornsdecker will go to extremes to stop the play do you," Mrs. Barnsworth asks.

"I have no idea what he is going to do next. I have lived with him for twenty-one years and I have never seen him act like this," Bessi says as she walks through the grass around the corner of the school building. "I think the dream's concept has him really stirred up."

"Well, if I was in his position, it might stir me up too," Mrs. Barnsworth says, walking through the large gates into the track area. "The kids are really proud of the new facility the town donated."

"I know and I hear it has caused some extra competition between the boys and the girls," Bessi says with a smile.

"It's funny to watch what goes on here between them. The girls of this generation have such a competitive drive, much more than I did when I was in school," Mrs. Barnsworth says as she steps up to the bleachers and sits down.

"I know, much more than I did, too," Bessi says, sitting down. "Well then, where do you want to start?"

"So I take it you are going to let Louisa and Lewis participate in the play?" Mrs. Barnsworth asks.

"Yes, I feel as you do about that. They can make their own decision," Bessi replies.

"I would like to get a more complete story than what I have heard so far," Mrs. Barnsworth says as she crosses her legs.

"Well, the dream started out in a kind of jungle-type setting and the devil was sort of angel-like at the beginning. After the incident with the monkey, lightning struck his wings and his hands became more pronounced somehow. I am not sure exactly how they changed; they just did," Bessi says as she watches some kids entering the track in the distance. "I could write the dream out for you if you'd like."

"Why don't you do that? It would be helpful to have a written account of the dream," Mrs. Barnsworth says with a smile.

"The dream seems kind of silly right now," Bessi says. "I hope you don't think I am strange for dreaming it."

"Actually, I wish I could have dreams like that. I don't even remember my dreams," Mrs. Barnsworth says. "Why do you think you have dreams like yours?"

"I suspect that it's part of the creative genes I inherited from my father. His side of the family was very creative and got most of their ideas from visions," Bessi says.

"I wish I had inherited a few more creative genes along with a few more IQ points," Mrs. Barnsworth says with a light chuckle. "My family was mostly actors and drama writers. I sometimes think maybe I jumped into teaching because I was to afraid of actually follow in their footsteps."

"I know what you mean. I jumped into having children and being a mother instead of following a creative career," Bessi says. "I sometimes wonder what I would be doing if I had just made a couple of different choices."

"Me too. Well, I need to get back to work. If you could go ahead and write out something, you can have Louisa or Lewis bring it with them to rehearsal," Mrs. Barnsworth says as she stands up and stretches her arms out.

"OK, I'll try and get it to you with in the next few days. It doesn't have to be well-written, does it?" Bessi asks with a smile.

"No, just something we can rewrite into a play," Mrs. Barnsworth says with smile. "You don't even have to type it out; just hand writing it would be fine."

"Great," Bessi says as she begins to walk along. "Thank you taking the time to talk with me."

"Oh, thank you. For a minute there, I felt like we were back in our school days. One of the perks to the job is that I get to relive my high school years everyday," Mrs. Barnsworth says with a smile. "And by the way, I wish you would call me by my first name, Wilda."

"All right but, only if you call me by my first name, Bessi," Bessi says with a smile and a light body rock back and forth as she walked slowly. "It is amazing that we can know people for so long and still not ever actually know who they are as a person."

"I know, it's that sad even in a small town like this, you rarely get to really know people," Wilda says with a smile and a tilt of her head. "Well, again, Bessi, thanks for the time spent I am going to cut through here and go into the gymnasium before I go to my office."

"OK, I'll get that outline to you soon. Good bye," Bessi says with a hand gesture.

"Good bye," Wilda says with a smile as she turns and makes her way through some gymnasium equipment stacked outside the building.

Bessi makes her way back to her car and sits for a minute. She begins to feel a sense of freedom that she had never felt. As she smiles, she starts her car and slowly makes her way through town over to Thelma's house.

At Thelma's house, she sees Thelma already pulling out damaged iris bulbs. "Hello, Thelma. Did that old geezer do a lot of damage?" Bessi asks as she closes the car door and begins to walk across the lawn.

"Would you believe that old fart took bites from nearly a dozen of them?" Thelma asks as she stands and straightens her back. "I shouldn't be doing this at my age, but I think it keeps me in shape."

"Well, for being seventy-six, you're in pretty good shape, old girl," Bessi says with a smile as she kisses Thelma on the cheek.

"I am sorry I woke you this morning from a pleasant dream," Thelma says with a shake of her head. "I wouldn't have minded if it were a bad dream."

"That is OK. I needed to get up anyway," Bessi says as she kneels down and moves of few of the iris leaves to see the damaged root area. "Oh my, what a big mouth that old gopher has."

"You're not kidding. That, that, oh, oh, I wish I new a few of those cuss words. I would curse that bucktoothed root eater," Thelma says gesturing with her trowel.

"Well, he'll get his someday. Life has a way of balancing things out," Bessi says with a smile.

"Doesn't it, though. That old saying 'what comes around goes around' is one thing I have been witness to being my age," Thelma says as she kneels back down and begins to slowly uncover more of the iris bulbs.

"It's amazing how life keeps track of everything that happens and counteracts in that way," Bessi says as she pulls out one of the damaged iris bulbs. "This one isn't going to bloom so we'll cut it back and let it heal."

"If that gopher keeps this up, I'll have to withdraw from the iris festival's competition," Thelma says as she continues to poke around with her trowel.

"Lets hope there'll be a few plants healthy enough to bloom a quality flower to enter in the competition," Bessi says as she moves the soil around several bulbs looking for damaged roots. "It would be a shame to come in second or third behind someone like Mrs. Cransford or Mrs. Musgrave."

"In the thirty odd years I have been competing, I never came in second to those women," Thelma says with a chuckle. "I wouldn't mind placing a ribbon after someone like Mrs. Mottweiler. God bless her soul."

"She does grow one heck of a pretty iris, that's for sure," Bessi says as she pulls up another bulb that had been eaten. "We could put a few of these damaged bulbs around that old gopher's hole and maybe he would get the message."

"That might not be a bad idea. If he gets hungry for one of my bulbs, he'll just eat one he has already ruined," Thelma says as she shakes her head.

"It's too bad that so many of these bulbs have been weakened like this," Bessi says.

"Well, I can't win that competition every year. I think it's been over seven years since I didn't place first for these red wine irises," Thelma says as she sighs.

"It is a rare color, kind of like you, Thelma," Bessi says with a smile.

"Me? Look who's talking, Mrs. Creativity," Thelma says as she looks around for more damaged plants.

"Actually, I don't see any more damaged bulbs Thelma," Bessi says, looking through the plants near one of the gopher holes.

"I guess that was the worst of it," Thelma says with a sigh. "We can do what you recommended and put the most damaged bulbs by his hole. Maybe he'll eat them instead of eating the others," she says as she stands up and straightens her back.

"All right, then I think there are two here that look pretty badly eaten, even though they could still send out roots sooner or later," Bessi says as she stands up and lifts the small bucket of iris bulbs. "I think I see the gopher's main hole over by the corner of the garage. I'll place these two bulbs there."

"OK. I'll head in to the house and get some tea started," Thelma says as she walks toward the garage with Bessi. "You can take the bucket into the garage and set them out on the work bench near the sink so their wounds can scab over," she says with a smile.

"All right," Bessi says as she steps quietly over to the gopher hole and begins to softly dig a small hole next to it. She places one of the bulbs into the whole then covers it up. After digging another on the other side of the gopher's hole, she does the same thing with the other damaged bulb. "Hopefully, you'll get the hint and eat these before you eat any of the others, you old coot," Bessi says with a smile as she stands and walks into the garage with the bucket.

"Bessi, I am out of green tea. Would you mind having a wild berry tea or mango madness?" Thelma asks from the doorway leading from the garage to the house.

"Oh, mango madness would be just fine," Bessi says as she sets out the bulbs out on the workbench. She then washes her hands in the sink and dries them off with a hand towel. For a moment, she stares out into the yard thinking about William, the gardener, and all that he has taught her about gardening over the years.

"Well, the water is getting ready," Thelma says as she steps into the garage. "Are you all right, dear?" She asks.

"Yes, I was just thinking about William and all that he has taught me over the years," Bessi says.

"You'll never get over him, will you dear?" Thelma asks with a smile as she pushes the button to close the garage door.

"I sometimes think that I should have married him rather than Silus," Bessi says with a nod of her head.

"Well, you sure have more in common with William than you do with Silus," Thelma says.

"I often wonder how things would have been if I had chosen to be with William rather than with Silus," Bessi says, following Thelma into the house.

"One thing is for sure, you wouldn't have those two wonderful children of yours if you had," Thelma says with a smile as she pours the hot water into the teapot to steep.

"Yes, I do have two wonderful children so I must have made the right choice," Bessi says as she sits down at the kitchen counter.

"And, that doesn't mean that you can't make another choice in your life to be with William," Thelma says as she begins to pure the tea into a cup.

"What do you mean? I can't just divorce Silus and run off with William," Bessi says with a chuckle.

"Why not? Lewis and Louisa will be going off to college soon and you will be free to pursue your own happiness. I have watched you for too many years be unhappy with your marriage dear and I think you should at least consider yourself for once," Thelma says as she sits down next to Bessi.

"I just can't divorce Silus because I am unhappy," Bessi says as she sips her tea.

"Why not?" Thelma says, sipping her tea. "I divorced my first husband after twelve years and married Arlo," Thelma says. "My first husband couldn't see past his own needs and thought the world revolved around him. I knew different, so I divorced him."

"I can't see myself just divorcing Silus without a good reason. I know I am unhappy, but life is about more than just my happiness," Bessi says with as smile.

"What makes you think that your happiness is not as important as his or anyone else's happiness?" Thelma asks.

"I just mean that I don't feel right making decisions based on just my happiness, that's all," Bessi says. "Especially when I don't blame Silus for my unhappiness."

"Well, you should start thinking about your happiness because once your kids are gone off to school, you'll be thinking a lot more about being unhappy," Thelma says with another sip of her tea. "Besides, I never did think much of Silus. He thinks he is God's right hand and that always rubbed me the wrong way. At least with William, he is more down-to-earth and much more of a man than Silus could ever be."

"William is quite wonderful and is definitely a different man than Silus. But, I can't compare the two and make my decision about which is better than the other," Bessi says, taking another sip of her tea. "If Silus was to do something to create a disturbance in our relationship, I could possibly make that change in my life."

"Well, he seems to be creating quite the disturbance over this dream ordeal, isn't he?" Thelma asks with a smile.

"Oh my, he is going totally bonkers. I wouldn't be surprised if he divorces me over this whole thing," Bessi says with a light laugh. "In all the years we have been married, I have never seen him be so disturbed over anything like this."

"In a way, I am glad his feathers are getting ruffled. He has gone around this town judging people in the name of God for too long," Thelma says with as smile and a shake of her head. "I know he is your husband and the father of your wonderful children, but that man has real problems and deep issues."

"He thinks he's doing the right thing. I can't judge him for that," Bessi says.

"Why not? He judges everyone else," Thelma says. "All I can say, dear, is that you deserve to spend the rest of your life with someone that loves you like William does and not like Silus thinks he does."

"I think Silus loves me in his own way. He just has a hard time showing it," Bessi says as she sips her tea. "I mean he tells me loves me and he is a good father. Just because we don't always agree on things, doesn't make him a bad guy."

"Being bad has nothing to do with it. It's thinking that he's always right and that no one else might have more insight than he has. He is selfish and self-centered, and I don't mind telling you that," Thelma says as she shakes her head.

"Thelma?" Bessi says with a smile.

"Well, I am sorry that man has rubbed me the wrong way over the years. He and his 'mightier than thou' attitude," Thelma says.

"I know what you mean, but he is my husband and I have to be more understanding than that," Bessi says. "We all have our faults."

"Yes, we do, and unfortunately his are some of the worst," Thelma says with a chuckle.

"Well, I must get home to do a few things. I do appreciate our discussion here today and I will give it plenty of thought. Sometimes I can't think of anything nicer than being with William. But, I can't let my self get carried off with some childhood lost love at this point in my life," Bessi says with a smile.

"You just keep thinking about that, dear. One day you just might find yourself doing just that," Thelma says, standing up and giving Bessi a hug. "Thank you for helping me today. I don't think I could have done all that and still had enough energy to get through the rest of the day. At my age, it is a big deal just being able to get dressed."

"Oh, you're in great shape for being seventy-six years old," Bessi says, hugging Thelma. "I'll call you tomorrow to check on things, OK?"

"All right, dear. I'll talk to you tomorrow," Thelma says, walking Bessi to the front door. "Say hello to the kids."

"I will, and I'll be seeing you soon," Bessi says, exiting the door.

"See you, dear," Thelma says, waving to Bessi as she gets into her car and drives away.

Bessi stops by the store and picks up a few things for dinner then drops by the church to give Silus the message about the book at the library. Silus is in a meeting so Bessi just leaves the message on his desk and continues on her way home.

At home, she puts the groceries away and puts the fabric she purchased in the den next to the sewing machine. She then proceeds outside where she spends over an hour watering the plants in her yard, small garden, and the new apple tree she had planted last week. When everything is watered, she returns to the house where she begins to lay out the pattern and fabric for the dresses.

Several hours pass and Louisa is the first to come home from school. "Hello, Mom," she says, giving her mother a hug on the shoulder.

"Hello, dear. How was school today?" Bessi says as she continues to pin together the fabric pattern's pieces.

"Oh, it was OK. Dad stopped by and gave me some books to pass around to some of my friends hoping that we will change our minds about the play," Louisa says with a sigh. "He doesn't realize that we have all made up our minds about the play and are even getting ready to cast the parts."

"I am sorry that your father is giving you such a hard time about the play," Bessi says.

"Which one of those fabrics is going to be my dress?" Louisa says as she rubs both fabrics with her hand.

"Which one would you like?" Bessi says with a smile.

"I like them both, but I'll take the yellow rose one, if that is OK?" Louisa asks, standing next to her mother.

"Well, that was the one I picked for you. I do need to know how long you want the skirt part and the sleeves," Bessi says as she continues to pin together cut patterns.

"Can I have the length about up to here?" Louisa gestures above her knee with her hand. "And the sleeve could be about here," She points to her upper arm with her other hand.

"Sure, what ever you want dear," Bessi says as she puts aside several cut pattern pieces. "I'll try and have your dress finished by Friday in case you have a date for Saturday," Bessi says with a smile.

"Mom," Louisa says with a shy gesture. "I need to go up to my room and read this story Dad picked out of the library's short story collection. It's about a young Indian boy named Hopping Crow. I told him I would at least read it for him."

"That would be nice of you to do that for him. He is trying very hard to get through this dream situation. Oh, that reminds me that I need to call this dream therapist he asked me to call. I hope it isn't too late. He'll never forgive me," Bessi says, setting aside the dress she is pinning together.

"You are going to see a dream therapist?" Louisa says with a smile. "Cool."

"Yes, cool. Your father thinks I need to see someone about my dreams so I told him I would do it," Bessi says, pulling out the telephone book and looking up the number of the therapist.

"Good luck, Mom. I'll be in my room reading that Indian story, OK," Louisa says, exiting the den and going upstairs to her room.

Bessi holds the phone for a minute before dialing, and then slowly starts pushing the buttons on the phone. "Hello, my name is Mrs. Hornsdecker, and my husband had spoken to you about me," Bessi says as she leans back into her chair.

"Yes, I remember. You're the one with the strange dreams," a man's voice replies. "I can see you Thursday morning at 10:15 if that works for you."

"Yes that would be fine. Where are you located?" Bessi asks.

"I am in a private home just across the street from the hospital on Oliver street. I'm in a blue house with white trim and the address is 774 Oliver Street," the man says.

"OK then, how much is this going to cost?" Bessi asks.

"Your husband has already taken care of that," he says. "However, if you have written any of your dreams down, you could bring them in so we can discuss them."

"Oh, OK," Bessi says. "So, then it's all set, I'll see you Thursday morning at 10:15."

"Yes, I'll see you then," the therapist says.

"Thank you," Bessi says as she hangs up the phone. She sits staring at the fabric in front of her trying to remember some of her dreams so she can write them down. After several minutes, she shrugs her shoulders and continues pinning together the fabrics.

"Hello, Mom," Lewis says as he enters the house. "You wouldn't believe what Dad's doing. He is passing out books with short plays in them to all the senior students," Lewis says as he flops down on the chair next to his mother.

"He is? I heard from Miss Wellsby at the library that he was checking books out and he had given one to your sister, but I had no idea that he was passing them out to all the students," Bessi says with a shake of head.

"They all think that he is nuts or something," Lewis says, looking at his book. "He gave me this book on Greek plays that I am supposed to read."

"He gave one to your sister, a story that is supposedly about a young Indian," Bessi says as she continues to pin the cut patterns together. "Well, try and be patient with your father. Maybe he will stop all this nonsense when he realizes it isn't doing any good."

"I hope so because we have already decided on the play we are going to do and there is nothing that he can do about it. We have already written the first act of the play and plan on casting the parts next Monday," Lewis says, standing up.

"Try and appease your father for now. It wont hurt you to at least read one of the Greek plays so he thinks you considered his feelings," Bessi says as she sets down the fabric for a moment. "Honey, just give your father some time to get past this behavior he has been displaying. I am sure it will pass soon."

"I hope so. He sure is making a fuss over nothing," Lewis says as he exits the den and continues to his room to read a Greek play before dinner.

"Well, I guess I better start thinking about getting dinner ready," Bessi says out loud to herself as she stands up and continues to the kitchen. "Oh, Silus, what are we going to do with you?"

"What do you mean by that?" Silus asks as he enters the kitchen.

"Oh, there you are, dear," Bessi says, startled by his sudden appearance. "I was just worried about you, dear. The kids say that you were passing out books to all the senior students today."

"Yes, I have been doing just that. If it weren't for your dream, I wouldn't have to," Silus says with a disapproving tone of voice. "I am trying to guide these students onto the right path instead of just standing by and seeing them make fools of themselves, wanting to put on such a demoralizing and perverted play as that dream of yours."

"Honey, it can't be all that bad. It is just a play and, besides, it'll probably end up as a comedy," Bessi says as she pulls out some pots and pans in preparation for cooking dinner.

"I don't want to discuss this with you, of all people," Silus says with a sharp voice. "Did you call Dr. Effenhart today for an appointment?"

"Yes, and I'll be seeing him on Thursday morning at 10:15," Bessi says as she shakes her head.

"Good, I hope he can do you some good," Silus says. "I'll be in my office until dinner. Please have one of the kids let me know when it is ready."

"Sure thing, dear," Bessi says as she shakes her head. She then pulls items out of the refrigerator to prepare dinner. "Let's see, we're having salmon, rice, and corn," she says to herself.

"Mom?" Louisa says, entering into the kitchen.

"Yes, dear," Bessi says as she straightens up from the refrigerator.

"I just finished that short story Dad gave me to read. I like the story but I don't think it would make for a good play," Louisa says as she gets a glass from the cupboard and fills it with water. "What am I supposed to tell Dad?"

"Well, tell him what you just told me," Bessi says as she begins to pull out the pots and pans from the cupboards.

"Oh, he'll just say something that will make me feel like I didn't give the story a chance or something," Louisa says as she sees her brother enter into the kitchen.

"Mom, could our family be considered a Greek tragedy?" Lewis says with a laugh.

"I don't think so," Bessi says with a smile. "Which Greek play are you reading?"

"Something tragic and depressing about some king and his disobedient daughter," Lewis says with a kidding gesture toward Louisa.

"Ha, ha," Louisa says as she drinks another gulp of water.

"Mom, does Dad really think that he can make us pick another play?" Lewis asks, stepping across the room and looking up the stairway toward his father's closed office door.

"He thinks that he has a chance to change your minds," Bessi says with a shrug of her shoulders.

"Do you think we should change our minds?" Louisa asks.

"No, I agree with your school and that you should make up your own minds about which play to do," Bessi says as she takes the salmon steaks out of their packages.

"I just hope Dad doesn't try something outrageous or something to try and get us to change our minds. I mean all the students are all set on doing the devil's monkey play, and that is that," Lewis says as he steps over to the sink.

"If you are sure about what you want to do, then all I can say is stick by what you believe in," Bessi says as she turns the flame down on the water for the corn on the cob.

"Thanks, Mom," Lewis says as he exits the kitchen.

"I just hope Dad can be as understanding as you are, Mom. I am going to go up and finish that story before dinner. I have a feeling that Dad is going to want a full report during dinner," Louisa says, kissing her mother on her cheek.

"OK dear, dinner will be ready in about fifteen minutes," Bessi says as she continues to cook dinner. While things are cooking on the stove, she sets the table and fills the water glasses. As the salmon begins to fully cook, she walks to the staircase and calls out to Louisa and Lewis that dinner is ready. "Could one of you please let your father know?" she asks with a sigh.

"Do you need any help putting anything on the table, Mom?" Louisa asks as she enters the kitchen.

"Sure, if you want to, put the glasses on the table. Then you could also put the corn on the cob in that blue bowl and place it on the table," Bessi says as she turns one of the salmon steaks over in the pan.

"Dad said he'll be down in a minute, Mom," Lewis says as he enters the kitchen. After Louisa places two of the water glasses on the table, he grabs the other two and carries them to the table. "I hope Dad isn't going to want me to talk about that Greek play during dinner,"

"I suspect he will want to say something about it," Bessi says as she begins to place the salmon steaks on a serving plate. "Just remember, kids, go along with your father's obsession right now and you'll be helping him adjust to the situation."

"I just hope things don't get any weirder," Louisa says as she sits down at the table.

"Me too. Dad has really been losing it lately," Lewis says as he sits down at the dinner table.

"Why do you say that?" Silus says as he enters the room and sits down at the dinner table.

"I mean, you're passing books out to our senior class," Lewis says. "How weird is that?" Lewis asks, lowering his head.

"I am sorry if that has embarrassed you at school. I am only trying to help guide your peers in the right direction before you all make fools of yourselves by doing some ridiculous dream as your senior play. This should be a well-thought and dedicated play that makes a statement about the integrity and moral structure of your classmates, not some whimsical display of insanity you all are making it out to be," Silus says as he watches Bessi place the salmon steaks onto the table and sit down at her chair.

"Dad, we all just think that this devil play would just be fun to do. We don't think we are being whimsical," Louisa says as she looks down at her plate.

"Well, you should all be ashamed of wanting to waste your time on such an immoral and disgusting concept as that dream represents," Silus says as he begins to dish up his dinner.

"It's just a play dad," Lewis says as he begins to dish out some food on his plate.

"Just a play? Have you read any of that book of Greek plays I gave to you?" Silus asks.

"Yes," Lewis replies.

"Those are just plays," Silus says. "Louisa have you read that story I gave to you to read?"

"Yes," Louisa says as she dishes up her dinner plate.

"Well, tell us about it," Silus says as he begins to eat dinner. "Isn't it set in New Mexico on an Indian reservation?"

"Yes. The story starts out kind of sad with a young Indian boy who is teased by his peers and cast out of the tribe. But a group of elders take him under their wing and teach him the old ways of the Indian tradition. The boy adapts and begins to get his confidence so he journeys into the wilderness where he discovers a life-giving energy of light that teaches him about his true purpose in life. The light of all life reveals to him the path in which his people can take to regain their spirituality and become a respected part of humanity again," Louisa says as she takes a bite of her salmon steak.

"Now, wouldn't that make for a wonderful play? It has inspiration, spirituality and humanity. Those are the things your school play should have in it," Silus says as he continues to eat.

"We are trying to write the play with some compassion and humanity, and it defiantly has a lot of spirituality," Lewis says as he takes another bite of his salmon steak.

"How can a story about the devil mating with a group of monkeys to create humanity have any of those things in it?" Silus says, looking over at Bessi. "We wouldn't have to even have this conversation if it weren't for you telling other people about your darn dream."

"I said I was sorry for being the cause of all this fuss. What do you want me to do?" Bessi asks, looking over to Silus.

"I wish you wouldn't be so passive about this situation and back me up on this," Silus says, taking another bite of his salmon.

"I told the kids that the decision was theirs and I stand by that," Bessi says, taking another bite of her food.

"I can't believe you. Not only do you go against me, but you encourage the children to pursue this damn idea for a play!" Silus says as he stands up and goes up stairs and into his office, slamming the door.

"Boy, Dad is really upset over this whole thing isn't he?" Louisa asks, looking at Lewis and then her mother.

"Yes, he is and I am sorry to be the cause of all this trouble," Bessi says as she continues to eat.

"It's not all your fault, Mom. Dad is just overreacting, that's all," Lewis says as he continues to eat.

"Well, I think the trouble is just beginning," Bessi says, taking a drink of water. "Your father is not going to accept the decision to do the play."

"I hope he doesn't go to extremes and cause more problems at school for us," Louisa says.

"I know. It was embarrassing when he went around the school passing out books to all the seniors," Lewis says, taking the last bite of his dinner.

"Let's hope he cools down," Bessi says. "He hasn't been feeling his normal self lately, so let's try and be supportive to him, OK?"

"All right, Mom," Louisa says as she stands up with her dinner plate.

"I'll try too," Lewis says, standing up with his dinner plate and then following Louisa into the kitchen. "I'll wash if you rinse and dry."

"OK, Mom did most of the clean-up anyway," Louisa says, returning to the table for more dishes.

"You both don't have to clean up tonight. I'll do that. Maybe you both could finish the stories your father gave you. It might make him feel better," Bessi says as she stands with her dinner plate and water glass.

"I'd rather do dishes than finish reading that Greek tragedy, but I guess you're right. It would make Dad feel better," Lewis says, finishing his water and setting the glass next to the sink. "Thanks, Mom."

"You're welcome, dear," Bessi says as she puts her apron on and begins running the dishwater, rinsing the dishes.

"I am almost done with my story anyway," Louisa says as she hugs her mother. "When I am finished with it, I'll let Dad know."

"All right, dear. Thank you for being patient with your father," Bessi says

"I just hope he is as patient with us and that school play," Louisa says as she leaves the room.

Bessi continues to clean the kitchen after dinner and put the leftover food into the refrigerator. She then goes into the living room where she sits in a chair and continues reading her dream book. After a half-hour later, she hears Silus enter into the kitchen. She goes into the kitchen and offers to get him something more to eat.

"That's all right, I will just nibble on the leftovers," Silus says. "I still have some work to do in my office so I won't be joining you in bed until late."

"Oh OK, dear," Bessi says as she watches Silus close the refrigerator door and then exit the kitchen to go up the stairs to his office.

"Oh well," Bessi says as she goes into the living room and gets her book. She then goes up to her room where she lies down and reads for a while longer.

Bessi is suddenly awakened by Silus getting into bed. She looks at the clock that reads one thirty in the morning. She gently rolls over and goes back to sleep.

The alarm goes off at a quarter after six. Bessi turns it off and then sets up in bed. After stretching, she goes into the bathroom and splashes her face with cold water. She then dries off with a hand towel and puts on her robe. Then she quietly leaves the bedroom. After starting the coffee, she sits down at the dining room table and begins to write down last night's dream.

"Oh, good morning, Mom," Lewis says as he enters the kitchen already dressed for school.

"What are you doing dressed for school so early?" Bessi asks with a smile.

"Some of the students are meeting in the cafeteria to work on our play," Lewis says as he pulls a box of cereal from a shelf.

"Good morning, Mom," Louisa says as she enters the kitchen and gives her mother a kiss on the cheek. "Did you have another weird dream last night?"

"Nothing too exciting to tell you about," Bessi says as she gets up and gets the milk out of the refrigerator for their cereal. "How many of the other students are going to be there this early?"

"I think most of the seniors are going to get there early. We are all eager to get the play in some kind of format so that we can begin to decide who gets which part," Louisa says, pouring milk over her cereal.

"Yeah, the sooner we get the play written out, we can start rehearsing," Lewis says, taking another bite of his cereal.

"Well, I hope this play is something you all are going to be happy with," Bessi says, pouring herself a cup of coffee.

"It is amazing how the whole senior class has actually agreed on everything regarding the play. There hasn't been one argument," Louisa says, eating her cereal.

"Just wait until the time comes when you all have to cast the play. Someone is sure to be jealous if they don't get the part they want," Bessi says, sipping her coffee.

"We have all agreed to choose the parts by pulling straws. No one can argue about their luck of the draw," Lewis says, finishing his cereal by drinking the milk from the bowl.

"Personally, I hope I get to play the part of the first human who learns how to communicate with the devil," Louisa says as she finishes her cereal.

"Louisa, can't you play something simple like a tree or something less antagonizing for your father?" Bessi says with a smile.

"A tree?" Lewis says. "I can see Louisa playing a tree," he says laughing.

"Who will be playing a tree?" Silus says as he enters the room. "And why are you two already dressed and ready for school so early?" he asks as he pours a cup of coffee.

"We were just talking about possible roles one could have in a play," Bessi says, getting up from the table. "What would like for breakfast dear?"

"Actually. I am going to have breakfast down at the diner with Minister Woods," Silus says. "Since half the seniors in the school belong to his church, I am going to ask him to help me persuade them to pick another a play. Even though I don't think it is going to do any good since I can't even persuade my own children."

"Dad?" Louisa says with a tilt of her head. "It's just that we all think that the story would make a great play. You'll see we'll turn the story into something meaningful."

"I find it hard to believe that you could make anything meaningful out of that ghastly concept," Silus says, shaking his head.

"You'll see, Dad. You're going to be proud of us and how we will work out the play," Lewis says, stepping toward the door with Louisa.

"So, I am to gather that the two of you are going to continuing this ridiculous play?" Silus asks.

"All the other students have already decided, Dad," Louisa says.

"That is not what I asked," Silus says with a head tilt.

"Yes," Lewis says with his head down.

"Yes, Dad," Louisa says with her head down.

"I can't believe my own children don't have enough respect for me to consider my wishes in this matter," Silus says.

"It's just that our school said that the seniors can pick their own play and this is the play we all want to do, Dad. We don't think that anyone but the seniors have a right to interfere," Lewis says, stepping closer to the door.

"Dad, you told us to do what we believe in and we both believe strongly that we can make a great play out of this story," Louisa says.

"How can you make something good out of something so demented and disgusting as that stupid dream?" Silus says, shaking his head. "I blame you for this, Bessi. I really do," he says, setting down his coffee cup and exiting the room through the back door.

"Mom, is Dad going to be all right?" Louisa says, looking out the kitchen window at her father driving away.

"I don't know, kids, but I have to say that I am proud of both of you for standing up for what you believe in," Bessi says as she steps over to Louisa and gives her a big hug and kiss on the forehead and then over to Lewis to do the same. "Just remember, if you two believe in this play, I support you one-hundred percent."

"Thanks, Mom," Louisa says, exiting the kitchen.

"Yeah, thanks, Mom," Lewis says, following Louisa.

"In the mean time, I'll try and deal with your father," Bessi says as she fills her coffee cup and sits back down to finish writing out her dream from last night.

About an hour later, Bessi drinks her last cup of coffee and finishes writing. She then cleans up the kitchen and goes to her bedroom to get ready for the day. After getting dressed, she decides to go outside and water the dwarf apple tree and the parts of the yard that the automatic sprinklers don't seem to reach.

When Bessi finishes the watering, she goes inside and begins to work on the new dresses she is making. As she continues to pin together pieces of fabric, the phone rings.

"Hello," She says, picking up the phone.

"Good morning, dear. It's Thelma. How are you doing today?" Thelma says.

"It's another day in the world," Bessi says while holding the phone with her chin against her shoulder. "I'm working on the new dresses as we speak."

"Oh wonderful, I can't wait to see them. I just called to check in and make sure that Silus wasn't giving you too much trouble," Thelma says with a pause. "Rumor has it that he is up to a few things."

"Well, he is reacting very strongly over this school play," Bessi says, taking the phone in one hand. "So much so that he stormed out this morning on his way to have breakfast with Minister Woods."

"Minister Woods? What in the world for?" Thelma asks in a surprising tone.

"Since some of the seniors belong to his church, Silus thinks that maybe he could have some influence on their decision to not use the devil and monkey dream for their play."

"Since when does the church think it has control over its flock?" Thelma says with a chuckle.

"Silus thinks that somehow, between the two of them, they can persuade the seniors," Bessi says, leaning back into her chair. "Silus doesn't realize that they have all made up their minds and started plotting out the play's scenes as of this morning."

"It might seem far-fetched, but it wouldn't surprise me if Silus doesn't have a bunch of church members picket the school," Thelma says with laughter.

"Don't say that. I think he just might do it," Bessi says, laughing along with Thelma.

"Well, good luck, dear. You're going to need it," Thelma says.

"Has that gopher done any more damage to the flower bed?" Bessi asks as she starts to pin together two pieces of fabric while holding the phone between her chin and shoulder.

"None that I can tell, but that little beast has time. It's only the middle of March, so he has time. I'll be lucky to even get a dozen flowers to enter into this year's event with all the damage that critter has done," Thelma says. "Well, dear. I'll let you get back to your sewing and I'll get into my yard. Oh, by the way what did you dream last night?"

"It was another odd one. I was lonely and upset in a strange land without any friends. I somehow planted a root-like thing and a friend started growing out of a shrub turning into a person. The person assured me that I would not be alone," Bessi says with a sigh.

"That was strange. You know, dear, you will never be alone because there are too many people who love you and care deeply about you," Thelma says.

"I know. I have no idea where that dream came from and why I would even have it," Bessi says, reaching for another spool of thread.

"All right, I'll let you go now. I will check in tomorrow," Thelma says.

"OK, have a good day in the garden, Thelma. Bye," Bessi says, hanging up the phone. She then begins to place two more pieces of fabric together and threads another needle with a light color thread. The phone then rings again.

"Hello," Bessi says, holding the phone with her chin and shoulder.

"Hello, my name is Mrs. Tonelli. My son Timothy is one of the seniors caught up in this play dilemma," Mrs. Tonelli says.

"Oh yes, I know Timothy and I think you and I have met several times at some of the town gatherings," Bessi says, taking the phone into her hand. "What can I do for you?"

"Well, I need your advice. I got a call from my church asking me to try and persuade Timothy to not participate in the senior school play. Now, I realize the play is strange but I don't agree with the way some people are overreacting," Mrs. Tonelli says with a sigh.

"I agree, Mrs. Tonelli. I too have the same problem. All I can say is that I told my children that if they believed in what they were doing, then, by all means, they should follow their instincts," Bessi says, leaning back into her chair.

"Your husband must be having a fit over that," Mrs. Tonelli says.

"He is actually having more than just a fit over this whole thing. He is totally overreacting and I have no idea to what extreme he will go in order to stop the play," Bessi says, shaking her head.

"You poor dear. How are you holding up with all this?" Mrs. Tonelli asks.

"It is not easy, but I am managing to hold onto my belief that these kids have to be able to make up their own minds," Bessi replies. "Besides, it has been a school policy to allow the students to pick their own play and I don't think they should have to change that policy now."

"Well, I am glad to have a chance to talk with you because I feel the same way. I mean, it's just a play. It's not as though they will be hurting anyone," Mrs. Tonelli says.

"I agree," Bessi says.

"OK, I will let you get back to what you were doing. I do thank you for taking the time to speak with me on this subject. You have helped me make up my mind to let Timothy make this decision on his own," Mrs. Tonelli says. "You take care now. Bye."

"Good bye, Mrs. Tonelli," Bessi says, hanging up the phone. She then takes a deep breath and continues working on her dress. She then glances at the clock near her work area and notices that she has a little over an hour before her appointment with the dream doctor.

After about forty-five minutes and several fabric panel pieces later, Bessi stands and stretches. She goes into the kitchen, washes her hands, and decides it is time to go to her appointment. She smiles as she looks out her kitchen window at her dwarf apple tree.

Arriving at the doctor's office fifteen minutes early, Bessi fills out appropriate paper work and then sits quietly in the patient waiting area. She is startled by a door opening and a younger male in his twenties exits the office.

"Are you Mrs. Hornsdecker?" a voice says from around the corner of the door where the doctor leans out into the room.

"Just give me few minutes and I'll be right with you," Dr. Effenhart says as he leans back behind the door and returns to his desk.

"Sure," Bessi says looking around at the empty waiting room trying not to be nervous.

"OK, I am ready if you are," Dr. Effenhart says stepping out from behind the office door. "You probably already know this, but I need to tell you anyway, I am Dr. Effenhart," he says holding out his hand to greet Bessi.

"Hello there," Bessi says shaking his hand.

"So, come on in and we'll get started," Dr. Effenhart says entering back his office and taking a seat in a large leather chair. "Go ahead and close the door behind you. You can take a seat in either of those chairs there," he says pointing across from him.

"Thank you," Bessi says looking around the room.

"Let me see if I can remember anything from my conversations with your husband. You have two children, twins who are seniors in high school."

"That's correct," Bessi says crossing her legs and holding her hands together in her lap.

"And, you have been having multiple dreams that bother you?" Dr. Effenhart asks.

"Yes," Bessi says.

"Well, I can start by explaining what some of the popular beliefs are on dreams and maybe shed some light on some dreams you may have in question," Dr. Effenhart says, picking up a pencil and note pad.

"OK," Bessi says. "I have been doing some reading about dreams and really don't have any questions about them. I am not sure why my husband wanted me to speak with you other than several of my dreams bothered him."

"You're probably referring to the dream about the devil and the monkey?" Dr. Effenhart asks.

"Yes, that dream has him quite shaken up," Bessi says.

"How do you feel about that dream?" Dr. Effenhart asks.

"I wish I knew why my mind dreamed it, along with other dreams. I don't seem to be so bothered by dreams like that so much any more. I try and just accept whatever I dream as just a dream," Bessi says.

"You are very creative, are you not?" Dr. Effenhart asks.

"Yes, I am," Bessi says.

"From what I understand about dreams, your active imagination never turns off. When you sleep, your mind is creating ideas based on fragments from your day-to-day life in reality. Your subconscious is trying to express itself by challenging the concepts you are exposed to day to day. Your inner mind is coming up with ulterior ideas to deal with your unsettled beliefs," Dr. Effenhart says.

"I can understand how that could be happening," Bessi says, relaxing her posture.

"For instance, if you are uncertain about, let's say your religious beliefs, then your subconscious will try and resolve the issue by acting out different ideas while you sleep. The level of creativity you have allows your mind the freedom to come up with some very different concepts from reality," Dr. Effenhart says, unfolding his legs and setting down his note pad.

"I think that is a fair explanation for what is happening. I don't think I want to do anything about it at this time," Bessi says with a smile. "I am learning to live with each night being full of dreams and strange realities."

"And there is no reason you should have to do anything about the situation. If anything, I would encourage you to relax even more about your dreams and just allow them to evolve. There is a chance that if your dreams cause you stress, I can prescribe some anti-anxiety medication, but I would recommend holding off on taking anything at this point," Dr. Effenhart says, looking over at his clock on the wall. "I had us scheduled for a half-hour consultation to start and that time is about up. I would be available to see you on a regular basis and discuss your dreams. However, with just our little time here today, I would say that you don't need that. I think you are handling things OK as they are."

"Thank you," Bessi says. "I'll keep you in mind if anything comes up and I need to discuss my dreams with someone," she says, standing up. "What do I owe you for this visit?"

"Your husband has already paid for the visit. With your permission, I'll discuss with him what you and I discussed," Dr. Effenhart says, standing up and stretching out his hand.

"That would be fine. You can tell him anything you wish," Bessi says, shaking his hand. "Thank you again doctor I will call you if I feel I want to discuss the dreams any further," she says exiting the room.

Bessi decides to drive by the nursery and see William and let him know the dwarf apple tree is doing fine. As she pulls up into the dirt driveway, William is helping load a few plants into a customer's vehicle. He stops to wave at Bessi as she pulls up and parks her car.

"Hello, Bessi," William says with a big smile.

"Hello, William. I just wanted to stop by for a moment and let you know that the dwarf apple tree is putting out new leaves," Bessi says with a smile as she turns to watch the other car drive away.

"Well, that is good news. You're still the only one in town with one of those trees. I decided to plant the other three I bought behind the nursery for my own use," William says walking up to Bessi. "It is sure nice to see you again."

"It is nice to see you again too, William," Bessi says with a smile. "Any new plant species I should know about?"

"None yet. I do expect to get a few in the first of April," William says waving at a car that honks as It passes. "I am sorry to hear about all the trouble on the home front over that school play."

"Word gets around, doesn't it?" Bessi asks, lowering her head. "Things will pass, I'm sure."

"Well, good luck with everything," William says as he takes off one of his work gloves. "Would you like to take a walk through the nursery with me?"

"I better not," Bessi says with a smile. "There is enough gossip going around town as is. I don't need to have people talking about us strolling through the vegetation together."

"You're too paranoid, Bessi," William says with a laugh. "But, you're probably right. You are the center of attention right now with that dream of yours."

"If it wasn't for my husband making such an ordeal about the seniors doing the dream as a play, things wouldn't be so bad," Bessi says, folding her arms.

"He'll get over it, and before you know it, this will all be behind you," William says beginning to walk away. "I need to get back to work, Bessi," He says with a smile.

"Yes, I need to be on my way. Thanks for the visit, William," Bessi says, walking over to her car. She turns while opening the door and waves at William, who waves back. As she drives away, they make eye contact again.

After Bessi stops by the store for a few things, she makes her way home. She spends the afternoon working on the dresses until Louisa and Lewis come home from school.

"Hi, Mom," Louisa says, entering the den where Bessi is working with the sewing machine.

"Hello, dear. How was school today?" Bessi says, kissing Louisa on the cheek.

"Just another day in the world," Louisa says.

"Hi, Mom," Lewis says with a low voice.

"Why so gloomy, Lewis?" Bessi asks.

"The play is only going to have twelve good roles in it and I just hope I get one of them," Lewis says as he kisses his mother on the cheek.

"Well, your chances are as good as anyone else's to get one of the parts," Bessi says. "Why are there only twelve parts in the play?"

"All the students agreed on the play outline and it only calls for that many characters," Lewis says as he exits the room to get a glass of milk from the kitchen.

"Well, it isn't too late for you all to pick another play," Bessi says to Louisa.

"We have less than three months until graduation and we need to start rehearsing as soon as possible. This morning, we all met early and pounded out an outline that we all agreed to. Tomorrow, we all pick straws to see who gets to play which part."

"Yeah, and for those who don't get a part, they get to play a tree or a cloud or even a bolt of lightning," Lewis says, returning with his milk.

"You both are pretty lucky. Maybe you'll get the parts you want," Bessi says, folding several pieces of fabric together.

"Dad asked me to read yet another short play. Why doesn't he understand that we have all made up our minds and we are doing the devil's monkey play?" Lewis says, taking a drink of his milk.

"He doesn't want to give up, does he?" Bessi asks, folding more pieces of fabric.

"Well, he'll have to face facts because we start rehearsing Monday," Louisa says, rubbing a piece of fabric with the palm of her hand. "This fabric has a nice feel, Mom."

"I hope it doesn't lose some of its texture after washing it. The shrinkage should be minimal," Bessi says, holding two pieces of fabric together.

"Mrs. Barnsworth asked me to ask you if you would be willing to do the costumes for this year's play," Louisa says.

"Don't I do them every year?" Bessi asks with a smile as she watches Lewis go back into the kitchen. "Don't spoil your dinner, now."

"She just thought because of the problems Dad was having over the whole thing, that maybe you would prefer not to make them," Louisa says.

"Well, let her know I will make the costumes no matter what your father has to say about it," Bessi says, continuing to fold together fabric pieces.

"OK, I'll let her know. The costumes so far are going to be a devil outfit and a group of monkeys," Louisa says. "There might be two angels that appear, but we are not sure if the parts is going to tie in with your dream."

"At this point, the play can take any direction you guys want," Bessi says.

"We wanted it to stay as close to your dream as possible. However, to allow for more students to participate, we needed more parts," Louisa says. "If we have two angels that convey God's views on what the devil did with the monkey, then that would be two extra parts. We even thought of having four angels appear together. There are even ideas to have a group of angels appear initially when the devil is first banned to Earth for his sins. The group of angels can escort him to the planet where he is to be confined and then they can all leave together."

"It sounds like you all have been seriously working on this play," Bessi says.

"Yes and it's been a lot of fun working out the details. Everyone has lots of ideas about the play and the direction it should take," Louisa says. "We left off trying to figure out how many monkeys does the devil initially mate with. If he mates with four or five monkeys, then there will be more parts for people to play. We are also trying to judge how long of a period should lapse before God punishes him for what he has done," Louisa says, standing up from the stool next to her mother's sewing table.

"It sounds like you all have your work cut out for you over the next few weeks," Bessi says, folding the last two pieces of fabric together. "There, now everything is ready to be sewn together."

"Great, I can't wait to wear this new dress to school," Louisa says. "Well, I need to get upstairs and do my homework."

"Yes, and I need to get busy preparing dinner before your father gets home, if he gets home," Bessi says with a smile and a stretch of her arms.

"What are we having for dinner, Mom?" Lewis asks as he enters from the kitchen chewing on a cookie.

"We are going to have a tuna casserole tonight," Bessi says as she stands up.

"Well, I'll be in my room doing my homework, Mom," Lewis says, exiting the den and going upstairs to his room.

Bessi goes into the kitchen and begins to prepare dinner.

About an hour passes and Silus enters into the kitchen.

"Well, I hope you're happy," he says, going over to the sink for a glass of water.

"What do mean, dear?" Bessi asks as she continues mixing ingredients in a large mixing bowl.

"I mean I hope you're happy that our children have gone against my wishes and are going ahead with this absurd play," Silus says as he takes a drink of water.

"You make it sound like I am happy that they went against your wishes," Bessi says, continuing to mix.

"You not taking my side in this issue means the same thing. That's how I look at it," Silus says. "You even stood by their decision to choose to do the play when you knew how much this whole thing has upset me."

"I only wanted them to make up their own minds and do what they thought was right. I don't see how you can turn that into anything else," Bessi says, pouring the ingredients into a baking pan.

"How else was I supposed to see it? You didn't consider what this whole thing was doing to me and the trouble it was causing me. I have no idea what made you backup their decision," Silus says, putting the glass down on the counter.

"I just wanted them to make up their own minds and I didn't understand why you were so opposed to their decision. It didn't make me happy knowing that you were so upset over this whole thing," Bessi says, placing the pan into the preheated oven.

"What are we having for dinner?" Silus asks.

"Tuna casserole," Bessi answers as she leans against the counter with her arms folded. "I wish you could just forget about this whole thing and let the students do their play, whatever it is going to be."

"I can't just stand by and watch them do such a horrible play especially when two of the students are my children," Silus says. "The whole concept is just wrong."

"And why is that?" Bessi asks.

"It's a sick concept that doesn't deserve to be given a second thought. Yet, these kids are going to bring it out into existence and rub everyone's nose in it like it was some classical drama. The concept is perverse and doesn't belong in our lives," Silus says, leaning against the counter on the other side of the room.

"I wish you could see it as less harmful than that. It is just a play, a fictional play with some ideas about religion. No one is going to get hurt by it, nor is anyone going to think any less of religion for it," Bessi says, shaking her head.

"Well, I've been affected by it," Silus says.

"Only because you are letting things get blown out of proportion for reasons that are still unclear to me," Bessi says, stepping over to the table and sitting down.

"It just so happens that this concept of yours challenges my belief in religion and since my profession is religion, this twisted concept has a profound effect on my view of religious possibilities. Also, it really bothers me that other people are going to be exposed to this twisted idea of human evolution. It just might confuse some people," Silus says, sitting down at the table.

"I understand your concern that someone might get confused over this concept. But, honey, it's a fictional idea. People are exposed to ideas like this every day of their lives. That doesn't mean we should all go around with our heads in a hole in the ground trying to hide from every concept that doesn't paint life as depicted in the Bible," Bessi says, folding her arms again.

"I know all that. I understand what you are trying to say, However, I think we have a moral obligation to not create obstacles that may prevent people from finding their way into religion. This play from your dream has that potential to lead people away from God's word," Silus says, folding his arms.

"I understand what you are trying to say, dear. However, this concept is so far-fetched that I think people are going to find it more unbelievable than anything else. And besides, the students are having an educational experience making the dream into something that will be entertaining and not so serious," Bessi says with a smile.

"Well, let's hope nothing more becomes of this whole idea. The sooner it is over, the better," Silus says as he stands up. "I need to go into my office and do a few things, call me when dinner is ready."

"OK, dear," Bessi says with a smile as she watches Silus leave the kitchen and go up stairs to his office. "Oh boy, sometimes that man," she says, standing up and checking the clock on the stove and then sets the timer. After wiping down the counter and rinsing out the mixing bowl, she returns to her sewing area and continues to work on the dresses.

Several minutes pass and Louisa enters into the room.

"Mom," she says, sitting next to her mother. "I overheard your conversation with Dad. Do you think he is ready to let us do the play?"

"I think so, but maybe during dinner you and your brother can talk about the play and mention some of your peers' good ideas," Bessi says, placing another pin into the fabric.

"I'll go talk with Lewis and we can work out what we are going to say to Dad," Louisa says, exiting the room.

After about a half-hour passes, both Louisa and Lewis return to the room.

"Mom, we decided what we are going to tell Dad. We decided that we should let Dad start the conversation and then we can respond accordingly. Since we don't really know if he is even going to let us continue with the play, we shouldn't be so willing to discuss the play unless Dad mentions it first," Louisa says as she looks over to Lewis who agrees.

"Yeah, we figure we'll let Dad say what he has to say and we'll hope for the best," Lewis says with a smile to his mother.

"Well, I think you both are being smart about the situation. Your father has come a long way toward accepting this whole idea," Bessi says as she continues to pin the fabric.

"All right, then I'm going back to my room and finish my math assignment. Call me when dinner is ready," Lewis says as he leaves the room.

"Yeah, me too. We are finishing up the last chapter of algebra this week," Louisa says as she leaves the room.

The buzzer goes off in the kitchen and Bessi puts down the fabric pieces and goes to take dinner out of the oven. As she sets the hot dish onto the counter, the phone rings. She takes off the kitchen glove and answers.

"Hello? Oh hi, Thelma. I'm just pulling dinner out of the oven."

"What are you having tonight?" Thelma asks in a light voice.

"Another casserole dish. Are you all right? You sound fatigued," Bessi says as she turns off the oven.

"No, I am not all right. I had a dizzy spell again and this time I fell down," Thelma says with a sigh.

"Are you hurt?" Bessi asks. "Do you want me to come over?"

"No, luckily I landed on the rug near the bed. I just called to ask if you would be willing to drive me to the doctor's office tomorrow morning? I have an appointment at ten o'clock," Thelma says with a light cough clearing of her throat.

"Of course I'll take you. Are you sure you're OK for tonight?" Bessi asks.

"Yes, I think so. I seem to have a lump in my throat and I feel tired, but I think I'll be all right. I have some leftover chicken pot pie I am going to eat and then go to bed early tonight," Thelma says.

"OK then. I will be over to pick you up around 9:15 in the morning," Bessi says.

"Thank you dear, I'll see you then," Thelma says, hanging up the phone.

After hanging up the phone, Bessi calls out to the kids, "Lewis, Louisa, dinner is ready." Louisa is the first down the stairs. "Honey, could you let your father know that dinner is ready?"

"Sure, Mom," Louisa says as she goes back up the stairs to her father's office. She knocks on the door then enters.

"Dad? Mom has dinner ready," Louisa says as she approaches her father typing on his computer.

"Alrighty, just let me finish up this letter and I'll be right down," Silus says, continuing to type.

"OK, I'll tell Mom to give you a few minutes," Louisa says as she leaves the room and returns to the kitchen. "Dad says to give him a few minutes to finish typing a letter."

"OK, thank you, dear. Could you take the salad to the table and ask your brother to fill the water glasses please?" Bessi asks.

"Sure, Mom," Louisa says, retrieving the salad bowl from the refrigerator. "Lewis, Mom said for you to take care of the water glasses," she says, setting the bowl on the table.

Lewis sets down his book and goes into the kitchen. After filling the water pitcher he returns to the dining area and fills the water glasses.

"Have you gotten past the quiz section of chapter twenty-seven yet?" Lewis asks.

"I just finished it before Mom called for dinner," Louisa says from his seat at the dining table. "I had to go back and rework some of the exercises to finish though," she says, watching her mother bring in the casserole dish and set it on the table.

"Oh good, you're just in time," Bessi says as Silus enters into the room. "I'll get the bread from the oven and then we will be ready to eat."

"What were you writing, Dad?" Louisa asks as she begins to put salad on her plate.

"A letter to the Trinity Evangelical Christian Church. I am writing Reverend Woods about your school play," Silus says as he passes the casserole dish over to Lewis.

"Oh," Louisa says as she looks over to Lewis who begins to put some casserole on his plate.

"I received a phone call just a little while ago from Thelma," Bessi says as she sits down at the table. "She has been having dizzy spells lately so she made an appointment to see her doctor. I'll be taking her in the morning," she says, placing some salad on her plate.

"I hope she is going to be all right," Silus says as he begins eating.

"Yeah, me too," Louisa says as she begins to eat.

"I have always liked Thelma," Lewis says in between bites. "She has a good sense of humor."

"Yes, she is funny at times," Bessi says with a smile. "I hope she is going to be OK."

"How long has she been having this problem, Mom?" Louisa asks.

"I think off and on for several months now. It seems to be getting worse," Bessi says, continuing to eat.

"Well, maybe the medical field can do something for her," Silus says, taking another bite. "How are things coming along at school, Lewis?"

"Fine. We are finishing up our algebra chapter this week and I hope to pass with an A," Lewis says, continuing to eat.

"And you, Louisa? How is everything at school?" Silus asks.

"Fine. I was voted the fastest female runner in the school and I think I can even run faster than most of the males in the school," Louisa says as she continues to eat.

"And the play, how is that coming along?" Silus asks as he looks over at Louisa then Lewis.

"Well, we are getting ready to cast the parts," Louisa says, looking over at Lewis.

"And what part are you hoping for, Lewis?" Silus says, looking over to Lewis.

"I am hoping to play the part of the devil," Lewis says as he looks down at his plate of food.

"And, Louisa, what part are you hoping to play?" Silus asks.

"I am hoping to play the female monkey," Louisa says as she looks over to her mother.

"I see," Silus says as he takes another bite of food.

"Well, there are not very many parts in the play," Bessi says as she looks over to Silus.

"They shouldn't be doing this play any way," Silus says as he reaches for a piece of bread.

"I guess I shouldn't be surprised that you both want to continue with your participation in the play. I would like you both to know that I am disappointed in you and hope that you understand that," Silus says as he stands up. "Thank you for dinner, Bessi, but I have a few things to take care of in my office," Silus says as he places his napkin on the table then leaves the room.

"Well, that went well," Bessi says as she takes a drink of water.

"He has never been disappointed in us before," Lewis says as he takes another bite of food.

"Yeah, I know. I feel kind of weird about it," Louisa says, looking over to her mother.

"Don't let it get you down, Louisa. Your father will get over it soon enough," Bessi says as she continues eating.

"I hope he doesn't get depressed over this," Louisa says.

"Don't worry, Louisa. Your father is strong enough to get himself through this, I am sure. Maybe it will even do him some good," Bessi says. "How about playing a game of Boggle after dinner?"

"No thanks, Mom," Lewis says. "I still have that math chapter to get through."

"Yeah sorry Mom, but I should study some more too," Louisa says as she stands up from the table and takes her plate into the kitchen.

"All right, I'll go back to sewing," Bessi says as she takes another drink of water.

"Thanks for dinner, Mom," Lewis says as he gets up from the table with his plate.

"You're welcome," Bessi says with a smile.

After Bessi finishes eating, she cleans up the kitchen and then goes into her sewing room to work on her two dresses. Several hours pass and Lewis interrupts her.

"Mom, are we doing the right thing by continuing with that play?" Lewis asks.

"I don't know. I mean it is something you both want to do and it doesn't hurt anyone, so I would say that it is OK to do the play," Bessi says as she reaches out and touches Lewis' arm.

"I just don't want Dad to continue feeling bad about it," Lewis says as he sits down next to his mother.

"I know, dear, but your father is just overreacting about the play and you should know that he will be all right. He may feel some frustration about you both doing the play but in no way are you hurting him," Bessi says with a smile.

"All right, I just don't want to hurt Dad over this whole thing," Lewis says as he stands up and kisses Bessi on the forehead. "I'm going to bed now."

"Good night, dear," Bessi says, kissing Lewis on the cheek. She then turns off her small sewing light and heads into the kitchen. "Oh, I didn't hear you come down," Bessi says to Silus.

"I thought I might have a few bites of ice cream before I went to bed," Silus says, licking a spoon.

"OK. I was just getting ready for bed myself," Bessi says as she washes her hands in the sink. "I was thinking about cooking a pot roast tomorrow. Does that sound good to you?"

"Yes it does. I was thinking about inviting Reverend Woods over to the house for dinner one night next week." Silus says as he gets a drink of water.

"That would be fine dear," Bessi says. "Maybe I can cook meatloaf that night."

"I'll let you know which night he says is good for him and his wife," Silus says as he leaves the room to go upstairs.

Bessi takes a drink of water from Silus' glass and then sets it in the drainer upside down. She then looks in the cupboard for a packet of dry pot roast mix and sets it on the counter. After looking in the refrigerator for other ingredients, she pulls a piece of paper from a drawer and makes several notations. She then prepares the coffee machine and sets the timer for automatic brew. After that, she turns off the light and heads upstairs to bed.

"Good night, Mom," Louisa says as she exits the bathroom across from her bedroom. "Do we have enough eggs in the refrigerator to have poached eggs for breakfast?"

"Sure. That actually sounds like a good idea. Good night, dear," Bessi says, entering into her bedroom and closing the door.

"I hope Thelma is going to be all right," Bessi says to Silus as she climbs under the bed covers. "Her health is declining."

"How old is Thelma?" Silus asks as he fluffs his pillow then settles down to sleep.

"I think she is seventy-nine years old," Bessi says as she turns off the light. "Good night, dear."

"Good night, honey. I love you," Silus says as he reaches over and kisses her on the cheek.

"I love you too, Silus," Bessi says as she returns the kiss then turns over to sleep on her side.

The alarm clock goes off at a quarter to six the next morning and Bessi reaches over to shut it off. With a stretch and a yawn, she sits up in bed.

"Good morning, dear," Silus says as he sits up in bed and then heads off to the bathroom.

"Good morning, honey," Bessi says as she slips into her slippers and heads downstairs. After starting the coffee pot, she stretches again and then goes to the front door to fetch the morning paper.

"Good morning, Mom," Lewis says as he makes his way into the kitchen.

"You are up and moving about early this morning," Bessi says as she kisses him on the forehead.

"I woke up around five o'clock and couldn't get back to sleep," Lewis says as he pours himself a glass of orange juice.

"Do you feel all right?" Bessi says, getting the eggs out of the refrigerator.

"Yeah, I feel all right it's just that my mind has been racing lately," Lewis says, drinking the rest of his orange juice. "What are we having for breakfast?"

"Your sister wanted poached eggs this morning. Would you like some too?" Bessi asks as she pulls out a pan from the cabinet.

"Sure, that sounds good. I'll be down after I get dressed," Lewis says as he heads back to his room.

"Honey, have you seen my blue plaid shirt with the short sleeves," Silus says as he enters the kitchen still in his pajamas.

"Yes, dear, it is hanging up in the laundry room. I just ironed it the other day and forgot to hang it back up in the closet," Bessi says with a yawn.

"How did you sleep last night?" Silus asks as he goes into the laundry room and then returns to the kitchen.

"I guess I slept OK. I don't remember any dreams, which is a good thing, I guess," Bessi says as she pours Silus and herself a cup of coffee. "Here, dear," she says, handing him the cup of coffee.

"Thank you. You're going over to Thelma's today?" Silus asks.

"Yes, I'll be taking her to her doctor's appointment. Then I think there are a few things around the house that she needs help with," Bessi says as she pulls out a large boiling pot for the eggs.

"Well, give her my best wishes and let her know that I'll be praying for her speedy recovery," Silus says as he leaves the kitchen to finish getting dressed.

"Mom," Louisa says as she enters into the kitchen. "Do you think this floral blouse goes with these plaid pants?" she asks, getting a large glass out of the cabinet.

"I think so," Bessi says, filling the pan with water and sets it on the stove's burner.

"How soon are you going to finish our summer dresses?" Louisa asks as she pours herself a glass of orange juice.

"Well, it depends on how much time I have to spend with Thelma helping her get through her illness," Bessi says as she pulls down some plates from the cabinet shelf. "Could you set the table, dear?"

"Sure, Mom," Louisa says as she gets the silverware from the drawer. "I hope Thelma is going to be all right."

"I do too, dear. I don't know what I would do if something happens to her," Bessi says with a sigh as she pulls out a loaf of bread and places two pieces in the toaster. "She is my best friend."

"How long have you known Thelma?" Louisa asks as she takes a drink of her juice.

"I think I knew her three or four years before you and your brother were born. I met her at the county fair where she had won the blue ribbon for her dialas," Bessi says with a smile. "She invited me over to see her garden and we have been friends ever since."

"Wow, that is neat. I hope I know my best friend for a long time," Louisa says as she takes another drink of juice.

"I hope you do too, dear. Having a best friend is like having someone always on your side and there for you no matter what happens," Bessi says as she begins to drop the eggs into the boiling water. "Could you get your brother and tell Dad that the eggs will be ready in a few minutes?"

"Sure, Mom," Louisa says as she leaves the kitchen. A few minutes later she returns. "Mom, if you need any help with Thelma just let me know, OK?"

"Thank you, dear. That means a lot to me that you want to help with Thelma. I'll keep you in mind," Bessi says as she places the toast on a plate then places three poached eggs on them. "Here you are, dear."

"Thanks, Mom," Louisa says as she takes her plate to the table and begins to eat.

"Here I am, Mom," Lewis says as he enters the kitchen.

"Just in time," Bessi says as she places two pieces of toast on a plate then places three poached eggs on them. "Here you are, dear."

"Thanks, Mom," Lewis says as he takes his plate to the table and begins eating.

"Sorry to hold things up," Silus says as he sets his briefcase on the counter.

"You're actually just in time, dear," Bessi says as she pours him another cup of coffee. "I'll have your eggs ready as soon as the toast pops up."

"Thanks, dear," Silus says as he takes his coffee to the table. "Anything exciting going on at school today, Louisa?"

"No, Dad, just another day of school," Louisa says as she continues to eat her poached eggs.

"What about you, Lewis?" Silus asks as Bessi places his breakfast in front of him. "Thank you, dear."

"Actually, Dad, a few of us guys are going to help Mrs. Millar clean her pet aquariums in her classroom," Lewis says as he continues to eat.

"Are you going to have to touch that tarantula?" Louisa asks.

"I think she has a small cage to hold him in until we get the big cage cleaned," Lewis says.

"What other critters does she have in her classroom?" Bessi asks as she sits down at the table with her poached eggs."

"She has several types of lizards, a snake, three types of spiders, a scorpion, and a young rabbit," Lewis says. "She really likes the rabbit. She found it wounded on her porch one morning about a month ago and she nursed it back to health. She says she might let it go in her garden when school is out for the summer."

"She should let them all go," Silus says, taking a bite of his breakfast. "How is the play coming along?"

"We are all excited to start rehearsals next week," Louisa says, taking another bite of her breakfast.

"Today we have the lottery to find out who will play which parts," Lewis says, taking a drink of juice.

"Well, I hope everything turns out in your favor," Silus says.

"Thanks, Dad," Louisa says.

"Yeah thanks, Dad," Lewis says as he smiles at his mother then over to Louisa.

"And, with all that said, I need to get to the church and you two should be getting to school," Silus says as he stands up with his plate and glass in his hand. "I'll just put these in the sink."

"Thank you, dear," Bessi says as she stands up smiling at Lewis and Louisa who are getting up and heading to the kitchen. "Can we all have a group hug?"

"That sounds like a good idea," Silus says as he puts out his arms and hugs the family.

"It's been some time since we have had a family hug like this," Bessi says.

"We should do it more often," Louisa says.

"OK, I can't breathe," Lewis says with a chuckle.

"OK then, thank you all," Silus says, rubbing the top of Lewis's head. "I hope everyone has a good day."

"Thanks, Dad," Louisa says as she heads upstairs to get her schoolbooks.

"Thank you, Mom and Dad," Lewis says as he grabs his backpack from the counter near the back door. "See you after school."

"We are very lucky to have such a wonderful family," Bessi says, hugging Silus.

"That we do," Silus says. "OK, now, I need to get to the church. I hope things go OK with Thelma."

"Thank you, dear. I hope she will be all right," Bessi says as she follows Silus to the base of the stairs where she watches him go up to his office for his brief case.

"See you after school, Mom," Louisa says as she comes down the stairs. "Bye, Dad," she says as she goes out the front door.

"All right then, I am on my way," Silus says, giving Bessi a kiss on the cheek. He then goes out the front door with Bessi closing it behind him.

"OK, now it's my turn to start my day," Bessi says as she goes into the kitchen. After putting the dishes in the dishwasher and cleaning up the kitchen, she goes upstairs and gets dressed. She then calls Thelma.

"Hello, Thelma, it's me. I just wanted to call and tell you that I am on my way to take you to the hospital."

"Oh good. I'll be waiting out front," Thelma says as she hangs up the phone.

Bessi gets into her car and drives over to Thelma's house. Thelma is outside watering an area of plants in front of the house.

"Hello," Bessi says as she steps out of the car.

"Hello, dear. How is the family doing?" Thelma asks as she walks over to the faucet and turns it off.

"Everyone is doing fine. We even had a family group hug this morning," Bessi says as she approaches Thelma.

"That is wonderful dear. Let me go in and get my purse and I will be ready to go," she says as she goes into the house. Several minutes later she returns and gets into the car. "I feel just lousy today."

"I am sorry to hear that Thelma," Bessi says as she backs out of the drive way and then continues driving down the street toward town. "What do you think is the matter?"

"I don't know dear, I just know that I feel fatigued, dizzy, and have no appetite," Thelma says, rubbing her hands together. "I felt nauseated this morning and I tried to eat but couldn't seem to swallow anything."

"That sounds odd. It's not flu season," Bessi says, turning into the driveway of the hospital and medical office building parking lot. "I'll drop you off at the entrance and then I'll find parking."

"Good idea, dear. I'll wait for you in the lobby," Thelma says, releasing her seatbelt and opening the door. "I hope I have the energy to make it into the office."

"Wait, I'll help you," Bessi says, getting out of the car and going to the passenger side to help Thelma. "Here, grab my arm."

"Oh thank you, dear. I seem to be getting worse all of a sudden," Thelma says, feeling her forehead with the palm of her hand. "I even feel a little temperature coming on."

"I'll take you into the lobby and then I'll park the car," Bessi says, helping Thelma into the lobby and over to a chair. "I'll be right back," she says, stepping over to the lobby information desk. "Could you please keep an eye on my friend until I get back here? I need to go park the car."

"Certainly, ma'am," the receptionist says, waving over to Thelma, who waves back.

"I'll be right back," Bessi says as she rushes out of the building. After a few minutes, she returns to the lobby. "Here I am. Parking didn't take too long."

"Thank you for helping me through this, Bessi. I don't know what is coming over me," Thelma says, standing. "I feel so weak and lightheaded."

"Sit back down. I'll go get a wheel chair," Bessi says, helping Thelma sit back down as she then goes over to the information desk and asks for a wheelchair.

"Yes, I'll call for one to be brought down," the receptionist says as she picks up a phone and request a wheel chair. "It will just be a moment and someone will be bring one down."

"Thank you, dear," Bessi says, going back over to Thelma and sitting next to her. "It will just be a moment. We are actually a few minutes early for your appointment so we have time."

"I like being early," Thelma says, resting her head in the palm of her right hand. "I just can't imagine what is wrong with me."

"It could be a flu type thing," Bessi says as she pushes back some of Thelma's hair behind her ear. "You have been lucky these last few years by not getting the flu."

"Yes, I have been very lucky, thank God," Thelma says as she hears the elevator doors open. She looks up and sees a man pushing a wheelchair. "Oh, thank goodness."

"Are you the one needing a wheelchair ma'am?" the man asks.

"Yes, she is," Bessi says as she stands and helps Thelma into the chair.

"Will you need help with her?" the man asks.

"No, I can get it thank you," Bessi says as she begins to push Thelma over to the elevator. "Just a few more moments and we'll be in the doctor's office."

"I hope they can shed some light on what is wrong with me," Thelma says, shaking her head.

"Let's hope so," Bessi says as she positions Thelma and the chair into the elevator. They go up to the third floor and out into the doctors office. "Hello, Thelma Frohmuth here for her ten thirty appointment."

"Hello, Thelma. How are you doing?" the receptionist asks as she stands with a smile.

"Hello, dear," Thelma responds. "I am not doing well. That is why I am here."

"Well, we'll get you fixed up in no time," the receptionist says as she looks at Thelma's chart. "There are no changes in your address or your insurance, are there?"

"No, I still have Blue Cross as my secondary insurance," Thelma says as she rolls her eyes back and looks at Bessi.

"OK, then you have a five dollar co-pay but I'll collect that after your visit today all right," the receptionist says as she places Thelma's chart on a rack for the office nurse who then picks it up.

"Come on in, Thelma," the nurse says as she opens the door to the exam room hallway. "We don't need to bother with your weight this time. You don't look like you feel very well."

"Oh, I don't feel well at all and I thank you dear for not putting me through any extra ordeal," Thelma says as Bessi pushes her into an exam room.

"Do you feel strong enough to get up onto the table?" the nurse asks.

"I'll try," Thelma says as Bessi helps her up and onto the table. "Oh, that wasn't so bad."

"So, tell me what has been going on?" the nurse asks as she closes the door and begins to take Thelma's blood pressure and temperature.

"I have been feeling horrible. I have been tired with some nausea. I haven't been eating very much and I am not getting a good night's sleep either,"

Thelma says as she lowers her arm with the blood pressure cuff on it. "I have been feeling light-headed and weak."

"Well, let's hope the doctor can fix you up," the nurse says as she finishes writing in Thelma's chart. "There is just one patient ahead of you. Then the doctor will be in, OK?"

"All right, dear. Thank you," Thelma says, closing her eyes and taking in a deep breath.

"Just relax Thelma," Bessi says as she sits in a chair next to Thelma. "Would you like a drink of water?"

"Oh that would be nice, dear," Thelma says, looking over to Bessi as she watches her get some water from a large bottled water dispenser.

"Here you go, Thelma," Bessi says as she helps Thelma raise up to drink the water.

"Oh, that was nice of you," Thelma says as she lies back down and closes her eyes.

"I'll set it down there on the counter for when you want more," Bessi says, sitting back down.

"Thank you, dear," Thelma says, taking in several deep breaths. "I hope it is not something serious."

"Try not to worry about it now," Bessi says as she strokes Thelma's arm with her hand. "Just try and relax and not worry about anything right now."

"All right, dear. I'll try," Thelma says with a smile as she lays there with her eyes closed and her hands folded over her stomach.

"Hello there, Thelma," Dr. Vootmeyer says as he enters into the room.

"Hello doctor, this here is my best friend Bessi," Thelma says, gesturing to Bessi.

"Hello there, Bessi. We have had the pleasure of meeting before," he says, shaking Bessi's hand. "So you're feeling under the weather, are you Thelma?"

"Yes sir, at least for the past several weeks anyway," Thelma says as she tries to sit up.

"You don't have to sit up," Dr. Vootmeyer says as he continues to sit and read her chart. "So, tell me what has been going on."

"Well, a few weeks ago I started feeling fatigued and sometimes I would feel nauseous for no apparent reason," Thelma says as she takes a deep breath. "I have also been experiencing a yucky feeling that seems to just overwhelm me."

"Do you feel faint when that happens?" the doctor asks.

"Yes, I do and I also feel a dull pain in my groin when that happens. But, these spells only last for a few minutes and then I feel better," Thelma says, looking over toward the doctor who is writing in her chart.

"I think we should run some blood tests and see if there is anything going on that will help us figure out what is happening," the doctor says, standing up and walking over to Thelma. "I am going to feel around your stomach for a moment, all right?"

"OK," Thelma says, closing her eyes and lifting up her blouse to expose her stomach.

"What do we have here?" the doctor says, feeling a lump in her abdominal area. "Did you know that you have this large lump here?" he says, feeling the lump with both hands.

"No, I didn't. But, since you have been touching that area, it is sore around it," Thelma says as she makes several facial expressions that reflect her discomfort.

"We need to get you over to the hospital for an ultrasound and see what is going on in there," the doctor says, stepping over to the sink where he rinses his hands then dries them off. "I'll give you a form to take with you and you should be able to get the test with in the hour. After the test, I want you to come back over here to my office. Although, if the test reveals something serious, then we'll have to admit you into the hospital from there."

"Oh boy, I hope it isn't something that serious," Thelma says, taking in a deep breath and lowering her blouse to cover up her stomach. "What do you think it is?"

"I don't know yet, Thelma, but this test will give us some kind of clue. I am also giving you a lab slip to have some blood drawn while you wait for the test .If they can get you in sooner for the ultrasound, then have your blood work after. But, either way, get it done and get back over here to my office. My staff will know what is going on and will make you as comfortable as we can until we get an understanding of what is going on," the doctor says as he fills out another form from one of the wall-mounted form racks. "Here is the form for the blood work and this blue form is for the ultrasound. Please get them done as soon as you can."

"Thank you, doctor. I'll go right over to the hospital and see what they can do," Thelma says as she sits up. "Do you have time to deal with all this, Bessi?" she asks, standing up and sitting back down into the wheelchair.

"Of course I do," Bessi says as she disengages the wheelchair brakes. "I have all the time we need to do whatever we need to do."

"Thank you, dear," Thelma says, patting Bessi's hand that rests on her shoulder. "You are a great a friend."

"I'll call over to the hospital and see what I can do to get you in there as soon as possible," the doctor says, opening the door and leaving the room.

"Well, let's get going then," Bessi says as she begins to push Thelma out of the room down the hallway. They exit the office and make their way to the elevator.

"Try not to worry, Thelma," Bessi says. "Chances are it could be nothing but a lump of fatty tissue or something simple like that."

"You're so kind to say that, Bessi," Thelma says, taking in a deep breath while she waits for the elevator. "I just hope it is nothing serious."

"We will know soon, dear," Bessi says, pushing Thelma into the elevator. "I think the radiation department is on the third floor in the main building right."

"I think so," Thelma says. "I was in there once a long time ago with Arlo when he sprained his ankle after he fell off the lawn mower."

"Oh yes, I had forgotten about that," Bessi says as the elevator door opens. She continues across the lobby where she pushes the button for another elevator that services the main hospital. The door opens and they enter. After several minutes, they arrive to the third floor and exit to the radiology department's front desk.

"Hello, you must be Thelma," a receptionist says as she reaches out for the form that Bessi passes to her.

"Yes, I am," Thelma says, folding her hands onto her lap.

"Great. Dr. Vootmeyer called to let us know you were on your way. It should just be a few minutes and we will take you back. You are lucky our eleven o'clock ultrasound appointment called and rescheduled."

"Oh, great," Bessi says, pushing the wheelchair over to the waiting area. "Isn't that wonderful that they can get you right in?"

"Yes, it is," Thelma says, taking in a deep breath. "I wonder how many ultra-sounds they do every day?"

"It would be interesting to know," Bessi says as she sits next to Thelma. "They will probably have me wait out here but if you need help, just let them know to come out and get me."

"All right, dear, thank you," Thelma says, patting Bessi on her knee. "You are a great friend."

"Thank you, Thelma. You are my best friend," Bessi says with a smile.

"Are you ready?" a nurse says as she approaches. "If you can just wait out here for now, I'll take Thelma back for the test."

"All right," Bessi says, sitting back down. "You'll be just fine, Thelma."

"See you in a few minutes, dear," Thelma says as the nurse begins pushing her into the testing area.

About twenty minutes pass and Thelma returns to the lobby. "I'm back, Bessi."

"Oh, that wasn't long," Bessi says as she stands up to greet Thelma. "Did everything go all right?"

"Thelma says that the doctor wanted some blood work done too," the nurse says as she engages the wheelchair brakes. "If you go back to the same elevators and go to the second floor, you will find the lab. When you exit the elevator, turn right and the lab is the fourth door on the left."

"Thank you, dear," Thelma says as Bessi unlocks the brakes and begins pushing Thelma toward the elevator.

"How did the ultrasound go?" Bessi asks as she pushes the elevator button.

"Oh, it was uneventful and painless," Thelma says as she takes a deep breath. "I hope the test reveals the problem."

"How are you feeling right now?" Bessi asks as she exits the elevator on the second floor and continues down the hall.

"I feel yucky and tired with a little nausea settling in," Thelma says with a shake of her head. "I hope I can go home and go to bed."

"Well, here we are," Bessi says as she opens the door to the lab and enters. "Hello, I am here with Thelma Orthendolph for some lab work to be done," she says, handing the lab form to the receptionist.

"All right, if one of you can fill out this information form and give me her insurance information, we can get started," the receptionist says, handing Bessi a clipboard with several pages to be filled out.

"Could you fill out the forms for me, dear? I don't feel up to it," Thelma says, placing her hand across her forehead. "I am getting a hot flash right now."

"Are you going to be all right to do the lab test?" Bessi asks as she kneels down next to Thelma.

"Oh, I'll be all right. I just can't wait to get home and lie down," Thelma says, reaching for the clipboard.

"No, I'll fill out these forms," Bessi says, standing back up and then sitting down in a chair next to Thelma. "Do you have your insurance cards with you?"

"Yes, they are here in my purse," Thelma says as she reaches into her purse and retrieves her wallet. "Just give her the cards and she will make copies of them."

"Great, most of this form doesn't apply to you, so I am almost done," Bessi says as she hands the clipboard to Thelma. "Just sign at the bottom there and the forms will be complete."

"Wonderful," Thelma says as she signs on the dotted line.

"Here are Thelma's insurance cards for copying," Bessi says as she hands the clipboard back to the receptionist with the insurance cards under the clip.

"Thank you, it will be just a few moments," the receptionist says, taking the clipboard.

"Just a few more minutes, Thelma," Bessi says, sitting back down next to Thelma.

"Thank you helping me out today," Thelma says, shaking her head and taking in a deep breath.

"Hang in there just a little longer," Bessi says, seeing a door open.

"OK, you can come back now Mrs. Frohmuth," the phlebotomist says from the entrance of the office area.

"Can I come back with her and push the wheelchair?" Bessi says as she stands up.

"Sure, we can draw her blood from the chair," the phlebotomist says with a smile.

"Are you ready?" Bessi asks Thelma.

"Yes," Thelma responds.

"All right, then here we go," Bessi says as she unlocks the wheelchair brakes and follows the staff back to the designated area.

"Just park her next to that large chair and I'll be right back," the phlebotomist says as she exits the area then returns. "All right, how are we doing today, Mrs. Frohmuth?

"Not very well," Thelma replies as she closes her eyes. "I hope you don't mind, but let me know when it is over so I can open my eyes."

"OK," the phlebotomist says as she prepares Thelma's arm with an alcohol pad and then she places the tourniquet around her arm above the elbow. She then places several different colored glass vials next to Thelma's arm and prepares the syringe and other supplies for the procedure. "OK, now you are going to feel just a light stick," she says, inserting the needle into Thelma's arm. "There, hopefully that wasn't bad," the phlebotomist says as she places the vials one by into the cartridge that allows the blood to fill the vials. "Almost done now."

"I will never get used to this procedure," Thelma says with her eyes still closed.

"All done," the phlebotomist says as she releases the rubber tourniquet from Thelma's arm and places a piece of cotton on the puncture site. "Please apply pressure to this area for a second until I get the tape on there."

"Sure," Thelma says, opening her eyes and placing her finger over the cotton ball.

"Thank you," the phlebotomist says as she places the tape across the cotton. "And you are all done. Your doctor ordered these tests stat so he'll have the test results within the hour."

"Thank you, dear," Thelma says, looking over to Bessi. "Are you ready to go back to the doctor's office?"

"Yes," Bessi says as she unlocks the wheelchair brakes, pushes Thelma out of the procedure area and into the lobby. "Are we free to go?" she asks the receptionist.

"Yes, you are," the receptionist says with a smile. "Good luck on your test results."

"Great, thank you," Bessi says as she opens the door and proceeds to the elevator. "That wasn't so bad."

"I hate having my blood drawn," Thelma says with a shake of her head. "I'll never get used to it."

"Me either," Bessi says, reaching the elevator and pushing the button. "Well, we will go back to the doctor's office and wait to find out about the tests."

"Thank you again for your help, dear," Thelma says as she enters the elevator.

"You're welcome, Thelma. I am happy to be some help to you," Bessi says as the door to the elevator opens and they exit.

"I hope they can find out what is going on with me," Thelma says as they continue down the hall to the business office elevators. After another short elevator ride, they arrive back to her doctor's office were they are taken to an exam room to rest and wait for the test results.

Forty minutes pass and the doctor enters the exam room.

"Hello Thelma, I am sorry to keep you waiting. Radiology faxed over the test results just a few minutes ago. The large mass is near one of your ovaries and may be cancerous. I am admitting you to the hospital for additional tests, maybe surgery and monitoring," the doctor says as he sits down and begins writing in her chart. "Do you have any questions at this time?"

"I feel overwhelmed right now. I don't know what to think," Thelma says as she looks over to Bessi who is lightly crying," "You stop that, dear, you'll have me crying in a moment."

"Sorry, Thelma, I can't help it," Bessi says, bursting out in tears. "Things are much worse than I had imagined."

"Yes, they are. However, we may be able to treat it if we have caught it early enough," the doctor says. "Can you make it back over to the hospital with your friend's help or do you want me to call over to the emergency room for some assistance?"

"We can make it on our own," Thelma says as she wipes some tears from her eyes. "Cant we?" she asks, patting Bessi on the knee.

"Yes, we've dealt with a lot of things together, we can certainly deal with this," Bessi says as she wipes her tears and takes in a deep breath. "Where do we go Dr. Orthendolph?"

"Well, I need you to take Thelma over to the emergency room. They will start doing some additional tests and get her admitted to the hospital. Let me finish writing out these notes and I'll give you a copy to give to the emergency room doctor. In the mean time, I'll get on the phone to several specialists that work with us and we'll work out a treatment plan. OK?"

"OK," Thelma says with a shrug of her shoulders and a deep breath. "What are my chances of surviving this?"

"It is too early to say right now, Thelma. Give me a few days and let me talk to the specialists before I answer you fairly."

"Thank you. I guess it was an unfair question," Thelma says with a smile as she wipes the tears from her cheeks.

"No, it is unfair that I don't have an answer for you," the doctor says as he stands up. "I'll makes some copies and be right back," he says, leaving the room.

"Hang in there, Thelma. I'll be here for what ever you need," Bessi says, kneeling down and hugging her as they both start to cry," Several minutes pass and Bessi leans back with her hands grabbing Thelma's hands. "Let's keep our chins up and keep in mind that people with cancer don't always die because of it."

"That's true," Thelma says, wiping her eyes. "My makeup is probably smearing."

"You look fine, dear," Bessi says, turning toward the door where she sees the doctor entering with paper in both hands.

"Here you go, Thelma. Just hand these forms to the emergency room staff and they will know what to do from there," the doctor says, handing her the forms. "Keep in mind, Thelma, that there is a chance that everything will be fine, all right?"

"Yes, doctor, thank you," Thelma says as Bessi opens the door and pushes Thelma out in the wheelchair.

"Just remember, dear, you are not alone," Bessi says, approaching the elevator. "I will do whatever it takes to help you get through this."

"Thank you dear," Thelma says, patting her hand on the wheelchair arm guide. "You are a true friend, Bessi."

"You would be there for me," Bessi says, entering into the elevator. "I think the emergency room is on the first floor and to the right of the elevator.

"Well, after I get settled, you better be off to take care of your family," Thelma says as she approaches the emergency room's front desk.

"Hello there. You must be Thelma Frohmuth?" a hospital staff member says from behind the counter. "Your doctor called us and let us know you would be on your way here."

"Yes, I am Thelma Frohmuth and I am here to be admitted into the hospital," Thelma says, wiping her tears from her cheek.

"Don't worry, Mrs. Frohmuth, we will take very good care of you. Let me direct you to a room and your friend can help you get into a hospital gown, all right?" the nurse says, stepping from around the counter. "Just follow me, please."

"Let's go," Thelma says as Bessi pushes her in the chair as they follow the nurse into a room.

"Here is a gown. Please put the opening in the back and place you garments in this large plastic bag for safekeeping. If you have any valuables, I recommend you give them to your friend to take home."

"All right," Thelma says, taking in a deep breath. "Thank you Bessi for helping me through this."

"You're my friend. I would do anything for you," Bessi says as she begins to help Thelma get undressed and into the gown. Several minutes pass and Thelma lies down on the bed. Bessi covers her up with a sheet and light blanket and she stands next to her holding her hand. "Thelma, keep thinking positively and try not to worry about things. I'll take care of your house as long as this takes."

"Thank you, dear. And, if you could open my mail and pay anything that needs to be paid, I will reimburse you later," Thelma says, closing her eyes trying to relax. "I guess I need to just wait and see what is going to happen.

"Hello there, Mrs. Frohmuth. My name is Dr. Cohigan. I'll be writing up your admission to the hospital. You regular doctor will follow you daily after you have been admitted," Dr. Cohigan says, stepping up next to her bed. "Do you need anything for comfort right now?"

"I do feel yucky with general pain in my abdominal area," Thelma says, taking in a deep breath.

"I'll have the nurse give you something for that. In the mean time, we will place an IV in you hand so we can administer medication during your treatment. I will keep you informed of what we are doing and if you have any questions, please don't hesitate to ask me or one of our staff. So, give me a few minutes and we'll have you feeling better, all right?"

"Thank you, doctor," Thelma says, looking over to Bessi. "You should run along now Bessi. There is no reason for you to hang out here."

"Well, I'll check in with you a little later then," Bessi says, patting Thelma on her shoulder and then kissing her forehead. "I will be back in a little while."

"Thank you dear," Thelma says. "You are a good friend."

"So are you dear," Bessi says. "See you later."

"Bye," Thelma says as the nurse approaches with a tray of IV implements and medication for pain.

Several hours pass and Thelma is drowsy and relaxed waiting to be taken for another test. One of the nurses enters the room. "Are you hungry, Mrs. Frohm-uth?"

"No, dear, I feel OK right now," Thelma says, repositioning herself on the bed. "What time is it?"

"It is almost three o'clock," the nurse says. "Your friend Bessi stopped by but you were sleeping. She said she would stop by later."

"Thank you," Thelma says, closing her eyes and taking in a deep breath. She slowly falls asleep.

Bessi is at home working at her sewing machine on the dresses. Louisa comes home from school.

"Hello, Mom, how was your day?" Louisa asks as she kisses her mother on the cheek.

"Hello, dear," Bessi says, setting down the fabric pattern she was pinning together. "My day was just fine. How was school today?"

"I got an A on my math test," Louisa says, looking at her finished dress. "You finished my dress."

"Yes, I finished this morning," Bessi says, stepping over to the dress on the mannequin. "Here let me help you try it on,"

"Oh, I can't wait," Louisa says with excitement. "It looks very pretty, Mother. Thank you for making it."

"You are welcome, dear. I just hope the costumes for the play turn out as nice as this dress did," Bessi says, slipping the dress over Louisa's head. "Turn around and I'll zip you up."

"Thank you, Mom," Louisa says, looking in the mirror as Bessi zips up the dress.

"Oh, it is beautiful, Mom," Louisa says as she turns from side to side looking in the mirror. "I can't wait to wear it to school tomorrow."

"I am happy you like it so much," Bessi says, hugging Louisa. "Now, I need to get back to work on the devil costume that I have been working on."

"Have you gotten all the fabric you need for all the costumes?" Louisa asks, stepping over to the sewing table.

"I just picked up the last of the fabric today after I visited with Thelma in the hospital," Bessi says as she continues to pin the paper pattern onto the fabric. "I wanted to do the devil costume first and next I'll do your monkey costume."

"Oh, I can't wait to try it on," Louisa says. "I'm going to my room now to get on the Internet and research the Hawaiian volcano god Palea for my reading class."

"Oh, that sounds interesting," Bessi says, pinning the fabric. "Maybe you can tell us about it during dinner."

"OK, Mom," Louisa says, exiting the room.

About fifteen minutes pass, Lewis comes home and enters the sewing room. "Hello, Mom," he says, kissing her on the cheek.

"Hello, dear, how was rehearsal today?" Bessi says, continuing to pin the fabric.

"Oh, it was fun but I can't wait until we get to the more complicated acting parts," Lewis says, sitting down next to his mother. "What are you working on?"

"This is your devil costume," Bessi says as she smiles and continues to work.

"All right. I can't wait to try it on," Lewis says, standing up and touching the fabric. "It feels soft."

"It is red silk," Bessi says. "And it wasn't cheap."

"It is going to look great," Lewis says. "I am going up to my room and work on my English essay."

"Oh, what is it going to be on?" Bessi asks.

"I am writing an essay on how society is impacted by religion and how diverse the religions are in our country."

"That should be interesting," Bessi says, beginning to cut the pattern out of the fabric.

"I think it is going to be a great piece of work, if I do say so myself."

"Good for you, dear," Bessi says as she continues to cut the fabric.

"I'll see you later Mom," Lewis says, exiting the room.

"I'll call you for dinner at about six o'clock," Bessi says loudly. She then finishes cutting the fabric and the phone rings.

"Hello."

"Yes hello, Bessi, this is Mrs. Gilsby from the hardware store,"

"Yes," Bessi says.

"I am calling about the foam board ordered for the senior school play," Mrs. Gilsby says.

"Oh great, I have been expecting a call from you," Bessi says with a smile.

"We were only able to get fourteen four-by-eight sheets right now. The company says it has several backorders and it will be another four days before we can get the rest of the order," Mrs. Gilsby says.

"That will be fine. Can we pick up the fourteen any time during your business hours?" Bessi asks as she continues to pin the fabric.

"Yes, we close at six p.m. daily," Mrs. Gilsby says.

"Great, I'll try and pick it up sometime over the two days," Bessi says.

"All right, thank you for the order," Mrs. Gilsby says, hanging up the phone.

"Thank you," Bessi says, hanging up the phone.

Bessi continues to sew the costume when Silus enters the room. "Hello, dear."

"Oh hello, Silus. How was your day?" Bessi says, standing up and giving Silus a hug.

"Well, it was a very tiring day," Silus says, taking in a deep breath. "It seems that everything seemed to be exhausting."

"I know what you mean, dear. Sometimes things just seem to weigh you down," Bessi says, walking with Silus to the kitchen. "We are having stuffed salmon with corn on the cob for dinner."

"That sounds great," Silus says. "I'll be in my office until dinner is ready," he says, exiting the room with a beverage from the refrigerator.

"I'll have one of the kids get you when it is ready," Bessi says, filling a pot of water. She gets the stuffed salmon from the refrigerator and begins preparing dinner. After about twenty minutes, she calls the kids for dinner and asks Louisa to get her father.

"What are we having, Mom?" Lewis says, getting a glass of milk to drink with his dinner.

"We are having stuffed salmon and corn on the cob," Bessi says as she dishes up the dinner onto different plates. "Did you wash your hands?"

"I'll do it now," Lewis says, exiting the room to the downstairs bathroom to wash his hands.

"Dad said he will be down in a minute," Louisa says, pouring herself a glass of milk.

"Thank you, dear," Bessi says, carrying two plates to the dining table. "Could you help me and carry two of the plates to the table?"

"Sure, Mom," Louisa says, picking up the two plates.

"I hope you like the salmon," Bessi says, getting two glasses of water for her and Silus.

"I love salmon," Louisa says, sitting down at the table.

"OK, my hands are clean," Lewis says, sitting at the table.

"Here I am," Silus says, entering the room and sitting down at the table. "This looks great."

"Thank you, dear," Bessi says, sitting down at the table and taking in a deep breath. "Let's eat."

"What new projects are you working on in your sewing room?" Silus asks, taking a bite of stuffed salmon. "This is great salmon."

"It is wild salmon," Bessi says, cutting a bite size piece from the stuffed salmon. "I have started working on the school's play costumes," she says as she takes a bit of food.

"Mom is working on the devil costume first, Dad," Lewis says as he takes another bite of dinner.

"I find it weird that my wife is making a devil costume," Silus says as he takes another bite of food.

"I can't wait for my monkey costume to be finished," Louisa says, continuing to eat.

"I can't wait until this play is over," Silus says, taking a drink of water.

"It will be over soon enough and before you know it the kids will be off to college," Bessi says, continuing to eat.

"Time sure has passed quickly," Silus says, smiling at Louisa. "It seems like just yesterday you both were starting high school."

"Finishing high school seemed to take for ever," Louisa says, taking a drink of milk.

"How is Thelma doing, dear?" Silus asks as he continues to eat.

"She is going through several treatments that are taking their toll on her," Bessi says, taking in a deep breath. "She is trying to cope with things the best she can. I think if things go well, she will be out of the hospital in four to five days."

"Are you going to try and help her at home or is she going to get an aide to help her?" Silus says, taking another bite of salmon.

"We haven't discussed that yet, but I am willing to help her any way that I can," Bessi says, taking another bite of food.

"She is lucky that she has you as a friend, Mom," Louisa says with a smile.

"Thank you, dear," Bessi says, taking a drink of water.

"Well, that dinner was great, Bessi," Silus says, putting down his fork after eating the last bite of food. "I don't know how you do it, but you are always making delicious meals for us."

"Thank you, dear," Bessi says, putting down her fork as she finishes her meal.

"Yes, thank you, Mom," Louisa says with Lewis saying the same thing.

"You are all welcome," Bessi says with a smile. "Don't worry about helping clean up tonight. You all run off and do something else tonight. I'll clean up."

"Thanks, Mom. I need to get back to my English assignment," Lewis says, standing up from the table and kissing his mother on the forehead.

"Thanks, Mom," Louisa says, standing up and taking dishes into the kitchen.

"I'll help you, dear," Silus says, standing up and taking his dishes into the kitchen, rinsing them before putting them into the dishwasher.

"Thank you both, but I could of done all that," Bessi says as she rinses her dishes and puts them into the dishwasher.

"I'll be in my office, dear, if you need me," Silus says, exiting the kitchen.

"I'll be working on my class assignment if you need me, Mom," Louisa says, exiting the kitchen.

"Thank you, dear," Bessi says as she finishes the last of the kitchen clean-up. She then goes to her sewing room and continues to work on the costumes.

The phone rings and Bessi answers it, "Hello."

"Hello, this is Thelma. I just wanted to talk to someone," Thelma says.

"How are you holding up, dear?" Bessi says as she sits back in her chair.

"I just feel terrible right now. The medication is keeping the pain to a minimum but I guess the side effects are nausea and fatigue," Thelma says, repositioning herself on the hospital bed.

"I am sorry to hear that you don't feel good," Bessi says. "I'll be in tomorrow to see you again. Is there anything I can bring you?"

"I can't think of anything," Thelma says. "Well, thanks for talking to me I feel better just hearing your voice. I'll see you tomorrow."

"All right,Thelma. I'll see you in the morning about nine o'clock," Bessi says, hanging up the phone. She then continues to pin some fabric together in preparation to be sewn.

Over an hour passes and everyone gets ready for bed. The kids both say good night and Bessi kisses Silus before she turns on her side to sleep.

The morning arrives and Bessi is the first to get out of bed. She makes her way to the kitchen where she turns on the coffeemaker. She then gets out a frying pan to cook eggs for everyone. She also plugs in the waffle iron.

Louisa is second to wake up and she goes into the kitchen and greets her mother. "Good morning, Mom."

"Good morning, dear. How did you sleep?" Bessi asks as she gets a glass of orange juice for Louisa.

"I slept OK," Louisa says. "What did you dream about last night?"

ιn odd dream," Bessi says, sitting down on a stool next to Louisa at the
.en counter. "I was watering the dwarf apple tree and suddenly it started to
.ow. I reached up into the tree to remove the price tag and the tree seemed to
pull me up on a branch. As it grew into the clouds, I could see the sun shining
through. Then apples started to grow in all kinds of colors and sizes. The
apples began to float around me and then they all burst into millions of dots.
Then I woke up."

"Wow, that was a cool dream, Mom," Louisa says, taking a drink of juice.

"Well, it wasn't a bad dream even though I am afraid of heights," Bessi says as
she gets up and takes some eggs out of the refrigerator and sets them on the
counter. "Are you going to wear your new dress today?" Bessi asks.

"I will," Louisa says, getting up and rinsing her glass before putting it in the
dishwasher. "I'll go and get dressed now."

"All right, dear. I'll call you when breakfast is ready," Bessi says, getting out a
spatula for flipping the eggs.

Silus then comes downstairs fully dressed. "Hello, dear. How did you sleep?"
Silus says, giving Bessi a kiss on the cheek.

"I think I had a good rest," Bessi says as she gets the waffle mix out of the pantry.

"No bad dreams?" Silus asks as he pours himself a cup of coffee.

"No, actually I dreamed about the apple tree growing like the beanstalk story,
but there was no giant in my dream," Bessi says as she mixes the waffle mix.

"I had a good dream last night," Silus says. "I was on an island with just you
and me. We walked along its beaches. It was a very relaxing dream."

"Sounds like a good idea for a vacation," Bessi says, pouring some batter into
the waffle iron.

Lewis then enters the room. "Good morning, Mom. Good morning, Dad," Lewis says, pouring himself a glass of orange juice.

"Hello, son," Silus says as he leaves the kitchen to get the newspaper at the front door.

"Good morning, dear. How did you sleep?" Bessi says, breaking two eggs into the skillet.

"I had a restless night last night. I was playing basketball yesterday and I think I did something to my arm," Lewis says, stretching out his arm and bending it with his elbow sticking out.

"Do you want to see the school nurse today?" Bessi says, lifting a waffle from the iron.

"No, I think the pain will go away. I just want to play basketball for awhile," Lewis says, taking a plate from Bessi that had a waffle and two eggs on it.

Silus enters the room. "The paper boy is running late today. There is no paper yet," Silus says.

"Honey, can you call Louisa? Breakfast is ready," Bessi says, adding more batter to the waffle iron and breaking two eggs into the pan.

"Louisa, breakfast is ready," Silus says from the bottom of the staircase.

"OK, Dad," Louisa says, exiting the bathroom and going into her bedroom.

"Here, honey," Bessi says as she puts Silus' waffle and eggs on the table. "I'll pour you some more coffee."

"Thank you, dear," Silus says, sitting at the table. "What time are you going to visit with Thelma today?"

"I told her that I would stop by around nine o'clock," Bessi says as she continues to cook two eggs for Louisa.

"Sorry I am late," Louisa says, entering into the room.

"You are just in time," Bessi says, putting the waffle and two eggs on a plate and handing it to Louisa.

"All right, this is my favorite breakfast. Thanks, Mom," Louisa says, sitting at the table next to her brother.

"Wow, that is a nice dress," Silus says, taking a bite of his waffle.

"Mom just finished making it yesterday," Louisa says, pouring syrup on her waffle. "Thank you, Dad."

"You're welcome. Honey, you did a great job. Are you going to wear your dress today?"

"I just might do that," Bessi says, putting her waffle and eggs on a plate. She then sits down at the table and begins to eat.

After breakfast, the kids head off to school and Silus heads off to his church. Bessi finishes her coffee and cleans up the kitchen. She then goes upstairs and puts on the new dress she made. As she walks out the front door, she picks several flowers for Thelma and she goes to the hospital.

It takes her about ten minutes to get there and she goes inside. "Hello, Thelma," she says, entering Thelma's room.

"Oh good morning, dear," Thelma says, sitting up in her bed eating breakfast. "I don't have an appetite but I am trying to force myself to eat."

"That is good. Try and eat as much as you can," Bessi says, kissing Thelma on the cheek. She pulls over a chair and sits down. "How did you sleep last night?"

"Awful," Thelma says. "But when I did sleep, I was dreaming about my mother."

"Was it a good dream?" Bessi asks.

"Yes, we were both knitting on the same blanket, sitting across from each other, and we were surrounded by wonderful flowers. I don't remember what we were talking about but I remember laughing several times."

"Well, your mother did have a good sense of humor," Bessi says with a smile.

"Yes, she did," Thelma says, trying to take another bite of her oatmeal.

"I dreamed last night that my new apple tree grew up into the clouds with me on one of its branches. The apples were wonderful colors and different sizes. I woke up feeling like it was a good dream," Bessi says as she looks at Thelma's food tray. "The fruit dish looks good."

"I think I'll try and finish that instead of the oatmeal," Thelma says. "Thank you for visiting with me."

"Of course, dear, and when you get out of here, I'll help you at home as well," Bessi says, patting Thelma on the arm.

"You are a true friend Bessi," Thelma says, taking a bite of her fruit dish.

"Thank you," Bessi says. "You didn't notice the dress I am wearing."

"Oh, I am sorry, dear," Thelma says. "I am not myself right now. Is that the dress you just finished making?"

"Yes and Louisa is wearing hers today," Bessi says, standing up and turning around so that Thelma can get a good look at her dress.

"It has beautiful colors and the style is 1920s, isn't it?" Thelma asks, pushing her food tray aside.

"I combined two different patterns and modified several pieces to have an original look," Bessi says, sitting back down.

"Well, you did a wonderful job. I wish I had had your creativity," Thelma says, repositioning herself. "Could you help me take a sponge bath? One of the nurse's aides said they would do it, but I just don't feel like having them do it," Thelma says.

"Of course I will. Do you want to do it now?" Bessi asks, standing up.

"If you really don't mind," Thelma says.

"I'll go get the necessary stuff from the nurse's station. I'll be right back," Bessi says, leaving the room. Several moments pass and she returns with a wash-cloth, a large plastic basin, and several large white towels.

"You are such a special friend, Bessi," Thelma says as she sits on the edge of the bed. "I am sorry to have put you through all of this."

"Don't be silly. What are friends for if not to help in time of need?" Bessi asks, stepping into the bathroom to fill the basin with warm water. "I'll keep adding warm water as it cools down."

"Thank you, dear. Can you close the door?" Thelma asks as she starts taking off her gown.

"Sure thing," Bessi says, closing the door. "Do what you can and I'll do what you can't reach."

"OK, dear," Thelma says as she starts to wash her shoulders and arms. "This medication makes me feel faint."

"Here, let me take over. You just sit there and save your energy," Bessi says as she soaks the washcloth and then rings it out. "Is the water warm enough?"

"It's just fine, Bessi," Thelma says, closing her eyes and softly shaking her head. "What will become of me Bessi?" she says as she begins to lightly cry.

"Now, now Thelma. Don't let this cancer get the best of you. We are going to beat this thing," Bessi says continuing to wash Thelma. "Remember, you come from a good strong bloodline and you're going to fight this illness."

"Oh, you always know what to say," Thelma says with a smile. "What would I do with out you?"

"I am proud to be your friend. Now, I'll let you do the other areas and we are all done," Bessi says, handing Thelma the washcloth after ringing it out.

"Thank you, dear," Thelma says, taking the washcloth and continuing to wash her personal areas. "I feel better already."

"Great, are you hungry at all?" Bessi asks.

"You know, I actually do feel hungry right now," Thelma says, slipping into a clean gown.

"I'll ask the nurse to bring in a few things to tempt your appetite," Bessi says, taking the basin into the bathroom to empty the water. "Is there anything that you are craving?"

"Jell-O sounds good," Thelma says, lying back on her bed and pulling the blankets over her.

"I'll see if they have any," Bessi says, leaving the room. After several minutes, she returns. "The nurse ordered a variety of snacks to be sent up from the cafeteria. She said it would take about fifteen minutes."

"Thank you, dear. I think I can hold out that long," Thelma says, taking in a deep breath. "Could you bring in my knitting supplies tomorrow?"

"Of course I will. Which project do you want to work on?" Bessi asks as she sits in the chair next to the bed.

"Maybe that green shawl," Thelma says with a smile.

"If you don't have enough green yarn, I'll stop and pick some up on my way in," Bessi says.

"I think I have an extra roll in my yarn box. But I don't remember right now," Thelma says, lying back and closing her eyes.

"Well, I better get on with my errands and I'll stop by later today with your knitting stuff, OK?" Bessi asks, standing up and leaning over to kiss Thelma on the forehead. "Try and think positively. We are going to get through this."

"Thank you dear," Thelma says, hugging Bessi.

"See you later," Bessi says, leaving the room. She stops at the nurse's station and thanks the nurses that are looking after Thelma. Then she leaves the hospital to do her errands.

After going to the school, she stops at the fabric shop and then ends up at the church at lunchtime. She and Silus go across the street to the senior center for lunch.

"Martha Warnock says they are serving chicken enchiladas today," Bessi says as she enters the crosswalk with Silus.

"If these enchiladas are anything like last year's, they will be a real treat," Silus says, waving to a passing vehicle.

"If they don't live up to your expectations, I will make you some," Bessi says with a smile as she finishes crossing the street. "I was thinking of having a ravioli night next week with fresh, homemade ravioli."

"Oh, I can't wait," Silus says, turning up the sidewalk to the senior center's entrance. "Hello, Walter," he says, greeting an older man at the door.

"Well, hello there, young'un," Walter says as he extends his arm to shake hands with Silus. "How is your world today, Preacher?"

"Just fine, Walter, just fine. I hear that you are going to turn eighty-nine next week," Silus says, shaking Walter's hand vigorously.

"Just another birthday, darn it," Walters says with a laugh. "I don't bother to count them any more. And how is your pretty missus doing these days?" he asks, looking over to Bessi who shyly smiles.

"I am doing just fine, Walter," Bessi says, shaking his hand.

"You better get in and get a plate. The seats are filling up fast," Walter says with a chuckle.

"I think we'll sit over near Glenda Miller and get an earful of what is going on out at the family farm," Silus says, continuing to walk into the senior center. Many people greet them as they make their way to their seats. "Hello there, Mrs. Miller."

"Oh hello there, Silus and Bessi," Glenda says, extending her arm to shake hands with Bessi and Silus.

"Well hello, you two," Gloria Weinholf says as she approaches with a plateful of chicken enchiladas.

"Hello, Mrs. Weinholf. Can we join your table?" Silus says with a smile.

"Most certainly," Gloria says as she sits down. "These look delicious."

"They sure do. Let's go get some before they run out," Silus says as he looks over to Bessi who agrees. "Save our seats now."

"We sure will," Glenda says, taking a bite of the chicken enchiladas.

While in line, Silus meets the town mortician, Greg Tobugen.

"Hello there, Mr. Tobugen. How are you doing?" Silus says, standing in line behind him.

"Well hello there, Silus. Nice to see you," Greg says as he shakes Silus' hand while he holds his tray with the other hand.

"I am doing just fine," Silus says, turning sideways to let Bessi say hello to Greg.

"Hello, Bessi," Greg says, shaking her hand with a big smile. "You get prettier every time I see you."

"Thank you, Mr. Tobugen," Bessi says shyly. "You always say the nicest things."

"How are the two kids doing?" Greg asks as he holds on to his tray with both hands. The server place a platter of food on his tray and he thanks her.

"Boy, oh boy, this sure looks good," Silus says as the server places the food on his tray. "Why don't you come over and join us, Greg?" Silus asks as another server places a small salad on his tray.

"All right, where are you sitting?" Greg says as he thanks the other server who places a roll on his tray.

"We are sitting over next to Gloria Weinholf," Silus says, stepping away from the service line. "Over there, in the red blouse near the wall with the calendar of events."

"Oh, I see her. Let me go get my jacket and hat, and I'll be right over," Greg says. He says hello to several other people as he walks over to where he was going to sit.

"I am starving," Bessi says as she approaches the table to sit. "I hope there are seconds."

"Me too, dear," Glenda says as she wipes her mouth with her napkin. "Me too."

"These are delicious," Gloria says with a chuckle. "I don't know why I never make them at home."

"Me either. I don't think I ever have made them," Bessi says as she takes a bite of salad.

"When Harold was alive, I think I made something close to chicken enchiladas," Glenda says with a chuckle. "I think my attempt got passed off as chicken and dumplings," she says with laughter.

"Oh, that's funny," Gloria says. "My worst cooking attempt was octopus soup. I didn't know that you need to clean them by taking out the guts and brains and stuff."

"Oh my," Glenda says with a chuckle. "Silus, tell us, what disaster has Bessi had in the kitchen when preparing a meal?"

"Well, let me see," he says as Mr. Tobugen approaches to sit down. "I think the worst thing was macaroni and cheese from scratch," he says, looking over to Bessi who chuckles.

"What's that?" Mr. Tobugen says as he sits. "Hello, ladies."

"Hello, Greg," Gloria says, taking another bite of food.

"Yes, hello, Greg. Glad you could join us," Glenda says, taking another bite of her food.

"We were just talking about cooking disasters and mine was macaroni and cheese from scratch," Bessi says with a smile as she takes another bite of food.

"Well, when my wife was alive she had the hardest time with homemade pies," Greg says, taking another bite.

"Oh, they are my favorite dessert to make," Bessi says, continuing to eat.

"I agree," Gloria says with a nod of her head as she takes another bite of food.

"I have a hard time with them too, Greg," Glenda says. "Mine are always runny or the bottom crust doesn't get cooked enough."

"I'll have you over one day this summer and I'll give you a few pointers on how to make a good pie," Gloria says.

"I am going to take you up on that," Glenda says. "And afterward, I hope I can make a great pie."

"My wife also had a hard time with things like chili and homemade soups," Greg says as he takes a drink of water.

"My chili never turns out well either," Gloria says, taking a bite of salad.

"The best chili I have ever had was out of a can," Bessi says with a chuckle.

"I agree," Glenda says. "And if it is that good out of a can, why go through all the effort and make it?" she says with a smile.

"So, not to change the subject, but, is anyone going on any trips this summer?" Greg asks as he takes another bite of food.

"Well, I am not sure if this counts as a trip, but I am going to take a day trip to our neighboring town, Mapleville, to see the new heritage museum open up," Glenda says.

"Oh, that sounds neat," Bessi says as she wipes her mouth with her napkin. "Didn't they remodel the old firehouse and make it into the museum?"

"That's right, they did," Glenda says.

"I think I read something about that in our local paper," Gloria says, placing her salad bowl on top of her plate. "If I remember right, the article said that this museum would have a gold miner that had preserved like a mummy."

"That wouldn't be somewhere I would want to go, just to see that," Glenda says. "However, there are enough other artifacts that make the visit worthwhile."

"I would like to see that exhibit," Greg says. "Did the mummy look real?"

"It did look real but it also looked strange, so I didn't stare at it to long," Glenda says, finishing her last bite of salad.

"I think that does count as a trip," Silus says. "I am hoping that we can get away someday for a vacation."

"Where would you go?" Gloria says, taking a drink of water.

"I don't know," Silus says. "There is nowhere I really want to be other than home."

"Me too, dear," Bessi says. "I have to say that if I was given a vacation, it would be right here at home."

"That's sweet," Glenda says. "You do seem like the homebody type."

"I personally would like to see Europe again," Greg says. "I liked all the people, museums, and the architecture. There is so much to see."

"I enjoy traveling by looking at picture books," Gloria says. "My husband, when he was alive, got me into that. We would spend all day flipping through books for hours and hours."

"That is a neat concept," Silus says. "The library must be filled with books with pictures of the world."

"Yes, it does," Gloria says. "When my husband was alive, we would pack a lunch and go into the library in the morning and come out that evening. We would pick a country and look at all the books the library had on it then pick another country and do the same thing."

"How sweet," Bessi says. "How long has it been since your husband died?"

"Two years in October," Gloria says. "I still dream about him."

"Good dreams?" Greg asks as he places his napkin on his empty plate.

"Actually, we travel sometimes," Gloria says. "The last dream I had with him was just the other night. We both were floating along like we were flying. We descended from the clouds and went to a farmer's market and touched all the vegetables and fruit," she says with a smile. "It was so real I am beginning to really believe that heaven exists. We get to be with our loved ones when we sleep and then finally when we die."

"Yes, I believe that too," Silus says. "I don't have a complete understanding of the dynamics of heaven. But, I am sure it exists and our souls are there as we sit here right now."

"I have dreams, too, with my wife," Greg says. "I wake up feeling like I had actually spent time with her in that spiritual realm."

"It is very possible that you did indeed visit with her while your body in this world was sleeping," Silus says, leaning back in his chair.

"I like the thought of my soul being with my wife," Greg says. "I sure hope it is the case."

"What did you dream about last night, Bessi?" Gloria asks.

"I was a visitor on a horse farm and out in a field a horse was giving birth. I watched the foal be delivered from the mare and then stand up," Bessi says, leaning back into her chair. "The odd thing was that the horse stood up on its hind legs and didn't have front legs. I remember telling someone who was also watching that the horse would make a good plow horse or a good riding horse with a special saddle."

"Oh, you have the oddest dreams," Glenda says with a smile. "What do you make of that dream Silus?"

"I don't know, I would guess that she really visited such a place in the dream world. That world is so vast and endless that anything is possible," Silus says. "Well, lunch was good but I have to get back to work."

"Yes, I have errands to do too," Greg says as he stands up from his chair with a stretch.

"I need to go by Thelma's and pick up her knitting things," Bessi says as she stands up and slides her chair in.

"Oh, I meant to ask about her. How is she doing?" Gloria asks, standing up.

"Yes, I meant to ask too but we were talking about dreams," Glenda says.

"She is going through several treatments that are taking their toll on her. But, I think she is taking it well," Bessi says as she begins to walk toward the door with the rest of the group. "I tell her you all asked about her."

"Oh, thank you dear," Gloria says.

"Yes, thank you, dear," Glenda says, taking in a deep breath. "Lunch was very nice."

"Well, you ladies have a good day and I'll see you tomorrow. They are having turkey meatballs tomorrow served over spinach pasta with mixed vegetables. Yum-yum," Greg says as he waves good bye as he makes his way down the front steps of the senior center.

"See you, Greg," Silus says then turning to the women walking down the steps. "See you ladies tomorrow."

"Good day, Silus," Gloria says with a wave.

"See you tomorrow," Glenda says, following her.

"OK dear, I'll see you after work," Silus says, kissing Bessi on the cheek. "Tell Thelma I am praying for her."

"Thank you dear," Bessi says as she walks away to her car. After she waves back to Silus, she makes her way to Thelma's house to retrieve her knitting things. She then goes back to the hospital and visits Thelma.

"Hello, Thelma," Bessi says as she enters her hospital room carrying her knitting basket.

"Oh good, you are here," Thelma says, sitting up in bed. "And you brought my knitting things. How wonderful of you. Thank you, Bessi."

"You're welcome. How are you feeling?" Bessi asks as she pulls over a chair next to the bed.

"I had one treatment this morning and I feel terrible. But, seeing you has made me feel better," Thelma says with a smile.

"I had lunch at the senior center with Greg Tobugen, Gloria Weinholf, and Glenda Miller. They all said to say hello to you," Bessi says, patting Thelma's hand. "Silus said he was saying a few prayers for you so maybe that will help."

"Thank him for me," Thelma says, taking in a deep breath. "How is my cat Tobu doing?"

"He is doing fine. I did find a dead gopher on the floor near the pet door," Bessi says, shaking her head. "I wonder if it is the one in the iris patch?"

"Oh, wouldn't that be wonderful. Unfortunately, that old gopher is smarter than Tobu so I fear he'll be around long after I am gone," Thelma says with a chuckle.

"Well, let's hope that you respond to the treatment so you can get back to your flower garden," Bessi says with a smile as she pats Thelma's hand.

"I hope I can get those irises to place this year in the flower fair," Thelma says. "Such a silly thing, but I sure enjoy the challenge of producing full blossoms."

"You are a master gardener, Thelma," Bessi says with a chuckle.

"It helps to have a good bulb-line to work with," Thelma says as she takes a drink of water from a plastic cup.

"Didn't you get the purple iris bulbs from your trip to Europe?" Bessi asks.

"Yes, when I went to Florence, I bought twelve bulbs from a German farmer," Thelma says with a chuckle. "I hade forgotten about that. It has been so long ago."

"Time does pass, doesn't it.?" Bessi says with a sigh. "Well, today I continue to work on the play costumes. I will bring in one of the monkey suits tomorrow to show you. I need to do a little freehand stitch work so I will bring it in and do it while visiting with you."

"Oh, that would be grand. I so much appreciate your visiting me so often," Thelma says, repositioning herself on the bed. "How many of the monkey outfits are you going to do?"

"Eight of them. Three female and five male," Bessi says with a tilt of her head. "I think I need to do a few things to make the distinction between the two. So I need to do some more thinking and experiments."

"You could make the shoulders wider for the males and you can have longer hair for the females," Thelma says with her hands gesturing.

"Good idea. I even thought about the males having a different hair color," Bessi says as she looks at the nurse just entering the room.

"How are you doing, Thelma?" the nurse asks as she approaches the bed.

"I am OK, under the circumstances," Thelma says with a smile.

"Is there anything I can get you?" the nurse asks as she checks the fluid bags hanging on the IV machine.

"I could use some green tea, if at all possible," Thelma says.

"I'll see what I can do," the nurse says as she smiles at Bessi. "Hello, Bessi."

"Hello, Margaret," Bessi says.

"Would you like some tea too?" the nurse asks.

"No, thank you. I am going to be leaving soon, but thank you just the same," Bessi says.

"Oh, and I see you've got your knitting basket," the nurse says as she steps over to the window and lowers the shade as the sunlight begins to come into the room.

"Yes, Bessi brought it in. I might as well be doing something productive," Thelma says as she reaches for the bag as Bessi lifts it to her.

"Let me know if you need anything from the store and I'll bring it in," Bessi says.

"I'll see about that tea," the nurse says as she leaves the room.

"Margaret is a nice nurse," Bessi says.

"I am lucky to have her," Thelma says as she pulls out some knitting needles and a project that she begins to work on. "Well, you better get on back to your sewing. I'll be all right."

"OK dear, keep your chin up," Bessi says as she kisses Thelma's cheek. "I will see you tomorrow, all right?"

"All right," Thelma says with a smile as she watches Bessi leave the room.

Bessi heads on home and continues to work on her costumes. After several hours pass, Louisa is the first to get home from school.

"Hello, Mom," Louisa says as she enters the sewing room. "I am only home for a few minutes to change my shoes and put on a pair of pants. We have rehearsals today and I want to be more comfortable."

"Oh, that's nice, dear. What time do you think you and your brother will be home?" Bessi asks as she holds up one of the monkey outfits. "What do you think?"

"All right, neat, Mom," Louisa says. "When I get home can I try it on?"

"Sure, why not? I can make alterations so it fits you," Bessi says.

"Great. I think rehearsal is only going to last for two hours so we should be home by five thirty or six," Louisa says as she leaves the room to go upstairs to change.

Bessi continues to sew and Louisa runs off to rehearsals. At five o'clock, Silus comes home.

"Hello, honey, how was your day?" Silus says, kissing Bessi on the head as she sits at the sewing machine.

"Great, I got a lot done," Bessi says, turning around. "How was work today?"

"I had a young couple from out of town come in to find out about getting married. Supposedly their preacher wouldn't marry them," Silus says as he follows Bessi into the kitchen.

"Are you going to marry them?" Bessi asks as she gets Silus a cup of tea.

"Well, I guess. They are both nineteen years old so I really don't have a reason not to," Silus says, sitting down at the counter. "They are going to make a nice couple and they both want to have kids. The guy woks for the local telephone company and she works for the hardware store as a clerk."

"It sounds like they might be in love," Bessi says as she places a cup of tea in front of Silus.

"They seemed very fond of each other and they said they were not going to have sex until they get married," Silus says. "I told them to come back on Friday and I will marry them."

"That is nice of you dear," Bessi says as she pulls some pork chops for dinner out of the refrigerator. "Would you like eggplant or squash with your pork chops?"

"Eggplant sounds good," Silus says as he stands up. "I need to do a few things in the office. Let me know when supper is ready. Where are the kids?" he asks as he takes a sip of his tea.

"They are at play rehearsal and won't be back until about five thirty," Bessi says as she starts to marinate the pork chops in a garlic and pine nut sauce.

"All right, I'll be in the office," Silus says, leaving the room.

Bessi washes her hands and then goes back to sewing for about twenty minutes. Then both Louisa and Lewis come home.

"Hello, Mom, we're home," Lewis says, entering the sewing room.

"How was rehearsal?" Bessi asks, turning around and getting a kiss on her forehead.

"It went really well and I think the play is going to be really cool," Lewis says. "How are the costumes coming along?"

"I finished three monkey outfits and need to make a few modifications to them once I know who is going to wear which one. If someone tall wears one, then I'll have to lengthen, and if someone short wears one, then I'll have to shorten."

"Cool, Mom. I'll try and get the teacher to cast the people who are going to be the monkeys so you can do what you need to do."

"Thank you, dear. Your sister wanted to try hers on tonight. Did she come home with you?" Bessi asks, standing up and exiting the room with Lewis.

"She is in the back yard with Tonya trying to act like monkeys," Lewis says with a chuckle.

"Oh, there they are," Bessi says, looking out the kitchen window. "They do look like monkeys."

"You said it, I didn't," Lewis says, getting a glass of milk. "I'll be in my room. Call me when dinner is ready."

"Yes, dear," Bessi says as she turns the pork chops over in the sauce. She then prepares the eggplant and gets dinner ready. As the pork chops finish cooking, she calls everyone to dinner.

"Hello, Mom," Louisa says as she enters into the house from the back yard.

"Hello, dear. You sure make a good monkey," Bessi says, pouring several glasses of milk. "Wash your hands and tell your brother and father that dinner is ready."

"OK," Louisa says as she goes upstairs. After several minutes, everyone comes to the table and they all sit down to eat.

"All right, pork chops," Lewis says, sitting down and beginning to eat.

"Thanks, Mom," Louisa says as she cuts her meat.

"You're welcome, dear," Bessi says as she continues to eat.

Several minutes pass in silence as they all eat.

"How was rehearsal?" Silus asks, breaking the silence.

"I really enjoy it," Louisa says, taking another bite of food.

"I enjoy it too," Lewis says, continuing to eat.

"I have three of the monkey outfits done and tomorrow I'll finish another," Bessi says, taking a bite of eggplant.

"I get to try my outfit on after dinner," Louisa says, taking a drink of milk.

"Well good. I am glad you are all involved in something," Silus says with a smile. "I am lucky you all have interests."

"Thanks, Dad," Lewis says.

"Yes, thank you, Dad," Louisa says with a smile to her father.

"Thank you, dear," Bessi says, continuing to eat.

After they all finish dinner, Lewis and Louisa clean up and do the dishes. Bessi goes into the sewing room and Silus goes back into the office. When the kitchen work is done, Louisa tries on her monkey suit and Lewis goes to his room to finish his homework.

About an hour passes and everyone gets ready for bed.

"Good night, Mom and Dad," Louisa says as she goes to her room.

"Good night, dear," Bessi and Silus say as they prepare for bed.

"Good night, Dad, Mom," Lewis says as he exits the bathroom after brushing his teeth.

"Good night, dear," Bessi says.

"Good night, son," Silus says as he closes the door to the room. He then gets into bed. "Are you going to read tonight?"

"No, I think I am tired enough to go right to sleep," Bessi says, kissing Silus. She then turns off the light and Silus does the same.

The next day Bessi is the first to get up, again. She goes to the kitchen to start the coffee and Louisa enters.

"Good morning, Mom," Louisa says as she pours a glass of orange juice. "I had a hard time sleeping last night."

"Oh dear, was it a bad dream?" Bessi asks, stroking Louisa's hair.

"No, I just couldn't stop thinking about the school play," Louisa says, taking a drink of juice.

"You are probably just excited about your part in the play. Try not to let it get to you," Bessi says, opening the refrigerator and pulling out a carton of eggs and a loaf of bread. "How about French toast this morning?"

"That sounds great, Mom," Louisa says with a smile. "What did you dream about last night?"

"I dreamed that I was in a Japanese garden with a large pond. I came upon an arched bridge where three animals were having a conversation. There was a bear, a turtle, and a giant crab. They were feeding cherry blossoms to some giant koi. When I approached them, they asked me if I thought that the koi had feelings. I tried to tell them that I didn't know but they insisted that I must know the answer," Bessi says, pouring herself a cup of coffee.

"Wow, Mom, you have the coolest dreams," Louisa says, drinking the rest of her orange juice. "I am going to get dressed now. I'll be down in a few minutes to help you with breakfast."

"Thank you, dear," Bessi says as she goes to the sewing room. As she sets out the pattern that she intends to work on today, Lewis enters. "Good morning, Mom."

"Good morning, dear. How was your night's sleep?" Bessi asks, picking up her coffee cup and taking a sip.

"I slept great and I even had a cool dream. I was in a soccer game with a group of little kids. I kept laughing with them as they tried to kick the ball. The ball kept shrinking and enlarging every few minutes. It was hard to kick the ball when it would keep changing size," Lewis says, kissing his Mom on the cheek. "I am going to get a glass of juice. I'll be right back."

"OK, dear," Bessi says as she continues to lay out the pattern pieces onto some fabric.

After a few minutes, Lewis returns to the sewing room. "When are you going to work on the devil costume?"

"I'll work on that next," Bessi says, picking up a notepad with several drawings on it. "Which of these designs do you like?"

"I like that one with the large horns and pointed ears," Lewis says, pointing at one of the drawings.

"Good, I'll make that one then," Bessi says, setting down the note pad. "I'll finish up this last monkey costume and I'll start your devil costume either later today or tomorrow."

"Thanks, Mom," Lewis says, exiting the room.

"Honey, have you seen my flower tie?" Silus says, entering into the room. "I feel in the mood to wear something different today."

"It is in the laundry room. I washed it after we went to that Chinese restaurant last month," Bessi says, kissing Silus on the cheek as he kisses her.

"Oh, that's right I got sweet and sour pork sauce on it," Silus says as he leaves the room. In a few moments, he returns. "You did a good job getting the stain out, thank you," Silus says as he ties his tie.

"You're welcome," Bessi says, taking another drink of coffee. "Anything interesting on the schedule for today?"

"No, just the regular stuff," Silus says as he turns to leave the room. "I am going to get some coffee."

"I decided to fix French toast this morning," Bessi says as she follows Silus into the kitchen. "How many slices do you want?"

"How about four pieces," Silus says, pouring his cup of coffee.

"I'll go ahead and start them now," Bessi says, getting a bowl from the cupboard and then breaking the eggs into it.

"I will be in the office doing paperwork," Silus says, taking a sip of coffee as he leaves the room.

"OK, dear," Bessi says as she whips the eggs and then starts heating the frying pan. Several minutes pass and she goes over to the base of the staircase and calls everyone to breakfast.

After everyone eats, Louisa and Lewis head off to school and Silus goes to work. Bessi finishes getting dressed and heads over to Thelma's house to feed the cat. Bessi then goes to the hospital to visit with Thelma.

"Good morning, Thelma," Bessi says as she enters the hospital room.

"Good morning, dear. How are you?" Thelma asks as she repositions herself in her bed.

"The question is, how are you?" Bessi asks as she leans over the side of the bed and kisses Thelma on the cheek.

"I don't feel so good," Thelma says, shaking her head. "The chemotherapy is really taking its toll on me."

"I am sorry to hear that," Bessi says, holding Thelma's hand. "Have you seen your doctor yet today?"

"No, he usually gets hear about ten o'clock," Thelma says, looking at the door as the nurse's aide brings in breakfast. "Great, I do feel a little hungry."

"We had French toast this morning," Bessi says, stepping out of the way and over to a chair where she sits down.

"I love French toast," Thelma says, pulling the tray of food closer to her. "More scrambled eggs and oatmeal."

"That is good that you have an appetite," Bessi says, smiling at the nurse's aide as she leaves the room. "What did they give you to drink?"

"Grapefruit juice and decaf coffee," Thelma says as she begins to eat her scrambled eggs.

"Has some of the nausea gone away?" Bessi asks.

"Fortunately, it has," Thelma says as she continues to eat.

"Well, today I finish the last monkey costume and start on Lewis' devil suit," Bessi says, standing up and walking over to the window. "I still need to get the red fabric today at the fabric store. Is there anything you need for your knitting project?"

"I am actually almost out of the color brown. If you wouldn't mind, when you are at the store, could you pick some up for me?" Thelma asks, leaning back and taking in a deep breath.

"I'll cut a sample of it to take with me to match it," Bessi says, stepping over to the side of the bed. She then gets out the brown yarn and scissors and cuts a piece. She then goes to the chair where she puts the piece of yarn in her purse. "Well dear, I am going to go now, but I will be back later today."

"Thank you, Bessi. And thank you for taking care of my cat Tobu" Thelma says, taking another bite of food.

"You're welcome," Bessi says, placing her purse over her shoulder. "Try and eat as much as you can."

"I will," Thelma says with a smile. "See you later."

"See you later," Bessi says, leaving the room. She gets in her car and drives to the fabric store.

At the store she talks to several people about Thelma's condition and then leaves. She then stops back by the hospital and drops off the yarn. Thelma was sleeping. When she gets home, she continues sewing, finishes the monkey costume, and starts drawing the devil pattern.

The end of the day draws near and the family is sitting down to dinner.

"The chicken tastes good, Mom," Louisa says as she continues to eat.

"Yes, you did a great job with the spices," Silus says with a smile as he takes another bite of food.

"Dad, Mom started my devil costume today and it looks really cool," Lewis says as he takes a drink of milk.

"Good, I am glad that things are working out," Silus says, taking another bite of food as he looks at Bessi.

"I am making the pattern from scratch so I hope it looks all right," Bessi says with a smile.

"Well, actually, I have no idea what the devil looks like. He may just look like a normal human," Silus says, taking a drink of water.

"I used the traditional image, horns and pointed ears with a tail," Bessi says with a light laugh. "I guess when I think about it, it is kind of silly."

"I agree." Silus says. "It is silly how people have developed the image. To some, the devil is evil beyond recognition and yet to others, like me for example, he looks like an angel but without the wings and halo. He looks like you or me, just condemned for eternity."

"Wow, I have never really given it much thought," Bessi says with a shrug of her right shoulder. "I mean, I have never formed an image of the devil, just a meaning to his name."

"Me either, I don't think they give you an image of him when you are in Sunday school," Louisa says as she takes a drink of milk.

"They just tell you that he was an angel that had fallen from heaven," Lewis says. "I had an image in my mind of him actually looking very handsome and wise."

"And he probably is," Silus says "It doesn't say in the Bible what he looks like. We have to leave it up to our imaginations."

"In my dream, he was a very handsome man," Bessi says. "I only made the costume to look like it does for a more visual effect. The acting part wouldn't be as effective with Lewis playing his part without a costume."

"That's true. People will pay attention to an image that is more dramatic and visually stimulating," Louisa says. "I think Mom's idea to dramatize the image is a good thing."

"Yes, I would agree for the play that it is appropriate to create an image that is going to catch people's attention. In reality, though, I would hope that we all can have a more realistic image of what the devil may really look like. I personally think he does have a human body and probably still has his angel wings," Silus says, placing his silverware on his cleaned plate. "I think I might use this topic in one of my sermons. I think it is important that we all have some image of the devil so we can deal with some of the complexities around his existence."

"In Sunday school, they say he lives in hell. Where is that?" Lewis asks.

"Some say it is the center of Earth, others say that it is in a realm similar to heaven," Silus says. "But, nobody really knows."

"Maybe it is one of the stars that we see at night," Louisa says. "I had a dream once that the stars were heavenly realms housing souls that didn't make it to heaven."

"That is a neat concept," Bessi says. "I like that. Instead of going to hell, a soul would go to one of the millions of realms where they would spend eternity. That would be a good reason why stars exist."

"You are saying that stars are realms that house souls?" Lewis asks. "That is weird."

"Yes, I think that if we don't go to heaven, but don't deserve to go to hell, then we get to go into one of the realms that best fits our soul," Louisa says. "We see the realms as stars but they are really worlds that house souls."

"We have some creative children," Silus says with a smile.

"Yes, we do," Bessi says as she laughs along with the rest of the family.

After a few minutes, they all get up and take their dishes into the kitchen. They all clean up and the kids go do their homework. Silus works in the office and

Bessi goes back to sewing. Several hours pass and after everyone says good night, they go to sleep.

The next day is like the day before. Bessi sends the kids off to school and Silus off to the church. She visits with Thelma and has lunch with her. Thelma's health is declining and Bessi starts to worry about it for the first time.

Bessi tries to keep herself busy by sewing but Thelma's condition really preoccupies her. She gets the devil costume nearly finished and has Lewis try it on for any last minute adjustments. Lewis is excited about the costume.

"Be still," Bessi says to Lewis as she tries to pin one of the legs on the costume.

"Sorry, Mom. I am just excited," Lewis says, staring into the mirror. "Grrrrrawl," he says to the mirror.

"Do you have to growl as part of the play?" Bessi asks as she adjusts the other leg.

"No, I was just doing it," Lewis says with a chuckle. "My part is actually simple. I talk to the voice of God a lot and I have several lines that I say to the monkeys."

"Well, I am glad you got the part you wanted to play," Bessi says as she stands up. "Now walk over to the door and back again."

"OK," Lewis says as he steps slowly.

"Great, I think that length is good enough," Bessi says as she goes over to her sewing table. "Go ahead and change back into your pajamas and I'll get those legs sewn tonight."

"Thanks, Mom, I'll be right back," Lewis says, leaving to go to his room to change. After several minutes, he returns. "Here, Mom."

"Thank you, dear," Bessi says, turning the legs of the costume inside out and beginning to sew.

"Good night, Mom," Lewis says, kissing his Mom on the top of her head.

"Good night, dear," Bessi says, continuing to sew.

After an hour passes, Bessi stops sewing and goes to bed.

The next few days go without incident except for Thelma's declining health. Bessi finishes the costumes and delivers them to the school.

"Hello, Wilda," Bessi says, entering the gymnasium of the school where the play rehearsals are held.

"Hello, Bessi," Mrs. Barnsworth says. "We are making great progress on the play."

"Oh, great. I hate to bother you, but I have finished the costumes and thought I might drop them off."

"Oh, perfect. I can't wait to see them," Mrs. Barnsworth says. "All right, class, I need a few volunteers to help Mrs. Hornsdecker bring in the costumes."

"I'll help, Mom," Lewis says with Louisa volunteering too.

Three other students follow Bessi out to the car. "Here, be careful with the devil outfit. It is in three pieces."

"This is so neat," Mrs. Barnsworth says as she watches the kids gently receive the costumes. "They look great, Bessi."

"Thank you, Wilda," Bessi says with a smile.

"Put them in my office on my desk," Mrs. Barnsworth says as she follows the kids back into the school and into her office. "All right," she says as the students carefully place them on her desk. "This is so exciting."

"I already got to try mine on," Lewis says.

"Great. You are so lucky to have a mom like you do," Mrs. Barnsworth says as she closes the door and locks it. "Thank you again, Bessi."

"You're welcome," Bessi says as she follows everyone back into the gymnasium. "Can I watch the rest of the rehearsal?"

"We would love to have you watch," Mrs. Barnsworth says. "All right everyone, we left off where the voice of God is condemning the devil for what he has done."

"Oh, dear," Bessi says with several of the kids laughing with her.

An hour passes and the rehearsal ends. Bessi drives Louisa and Lewis home. "I am so proud of you two."

"Thanks Mom, we are proud of you too," Louisa says with Lewis agreeing.

"Tonight, for dinner we are going to have vegetarian meatloaf," Bessi says as she pulls into the driveway to their home.

"I'll get the table set," Lewis says as he exits the car.

"Thank you dear," Bessi says, exiting the car. She then makes her way into the house and into the kitchen where she washes her hands. "Louisa, tell your father that dinner will be ready in ten minutes."

"OK, Mom," Louisa says, going upstairs.

Dinner goes well with good family conversation and then everyone cleans up and heads off to bed.

The next week goes by and Thelma is not responding to treatment and takes a turn for the worse. Bessi is spending more time in the hospital visiting with her.

Both Lewis and Louisa perfect their roles as opening night approaches, only one week away. Silus lets them know that several of the church members are going to picket the play's opening night in protest of its anti-religious sentiment.

Bessi tries to smooth things over but can't change the minds of several of the church members. She has a confrontation at the grocery store.

"I am sorry that you feel that way, Mrs. Johnson," Bessi says with a cantaloupe in her hand.

"Well, if you didn't have such dreams, then none of us would be in this situation," Mrs. Johnson says, putting a cantaloupe down and pushing her grocery cart down the aisle.

"Oh my goodness," Mrs. Ornackle says with a smile. "Don't let her get to you, Bessi."

"Thank you, Moreen," Bessi says, putting the cantaloupe in her cart. "I just don't know why people have to be that way."

"I don't know either," Moreen says, pushing her cart alongside Bessi's cart. "Oh, I found this great recipe in a cooking magazine for pine nut soup."

"Pine nuts?" Bessi says with raised eyebrows. "I haven't seen a pine nut for years."

"My Aunt Wilma sent me several pounds. I'll give you some," Moreen says, grabbing a loaf bread from the shelf.

"What else is in the soup?" Bessi asks as she grabs a loaf of multi-grain bread.

"Okra, mushroom, onion, and diced octopus," Moreen says with a shake of her head. "I substituted the octopus for shrimp."

"Good idea. I doubt we could get octopus here anyway," Bessi says, continuing to push her cart down the aisle. "If I get a chance, I'll swing by and copy down the recipe."

"I'll make you a copy and drop it by the house," Moreen says, grabbing a gallon milk from the refrigerated cooler.

"Great, thank you," Bessi says, getting two gallons of milk. "If you get a chance, stop by and see Thelma at the hospital. She needs cheering up."

"I will. I just didn't want to bother her," Moreen says, pulling up to the checkout stand.

"I understand but she would like the visit," Bessi says, placing the items onto the conveyer belt. "If you would like, I will be there this afternoon, if you would want to stop by around three o'clock."

"Oh, I would feel better if you were there," Moreen says as she waits for Bessi to empty her cart. "It's just that I feel uncomfortable being there by myself."

"I'll be there around three o'clock so we can meet in the lobby near the flower shop next to the elevators," Bessi says, swiping her credit card and punching in her code.

"Thank you, Bessi. I will meet you there then at three," Moreen says as she empties her cart onto the conveyer belt.

"See you then, Moreen. Thank you for the visit," Bessi says as she places the receipt in her purse and pushes her cart to the car. After loading and waving to another car that honks at her, Bessi goes home.

Bessi puts away the groceries and then goes back to sewing. Several hours pass and then she drives to the hospital where she meets Moreen in the lobby.

"Hello, Moreen."

"Hello again, Bessi," Moreen says, rubbing her hands together. "I feel so nervous."

"Try and relax. Just try and keep a positive attitude," Bessi says, entering the elevator. "She gets tired easily so we'll make the visit short."

"OK, I will try and talk about positive things," Moreen says. "I know, I'll talk about my irises and ask about hers."

"OK, here we are," Bessi says, stepping out of the elevator. "Hello," she says to the nurse at the nurse's station. "How is she doing?"

"She just woke up from a nap, so this should be a good time to visit," the nurse says with a smile.

"Oh good," Bessi says, stepping down the hall and then into Thelma's room. "Hello, dear," she says, approaching Thelma and giving her a kiss on her forehead.

"Oh my, look who is here," Thelma says with a smile as she greets Moreen with a shake of her hand.

"Hello, Thelma. I am sorry that you have to deal with such a horrible thing," Moreen says with teary eyes as she shakes Thelma's hand.

"So glad you came to see me," Thelma says, shifting herself on the bed. "What a unexpected surprise."

"Well, I met Bessi in the store and she said it would be OK to visit," Moreen says, looking over to Bessi then back over to Thelma.

"Thank you, dear," Thelma says with a smile.

"I was telling Bessi about this pine nut and octopus soup in the latest cooking magazine. I could make some and bring it in," Moreen says with a smile. "Although, I changed the ingredients from octopus to shrimp."

"A good choice," Thelma says with a chuckle. "I would love to try it."

"Oh great, that would give me something to do for you," Moreen says with a tilt of her head. "I'll make it tomorrow and drop it by Bessi's house. Actually, I'll make enough for you too, Bessi."

"Thank you, Moreen, but you don't have to do that," Bessi says, shaking her head.

"Oh, but I want to, please," Moreen says, taking in a deep breath. "Is there anything I can do for you, Thelma?"

"No, dear. Bessi is seeing to my house while I'm gone and the hospital is doing a good job treating me," Thelma says, closing her eyes for a moment.

"We won't stay long, Thelma. We just wanted to stop by and say hello," Bessi says, patting Thelma's hand. "I finished the costumes and dropped them off."

"Oh, I would have loved to have seen them," Thelma says.

"You'll see them opening night," Bessi says.

"I wish I could, but I don't think I will be out of here by that time," Thelma says, shaking her head. "Why don't you take pictures for me?"

"OK, I'll do that," Bessi says. "Well, we are going to leave now so you can get more rest."

"Yes, we should leave now," Moreen says. "You get better, you hear."

"All right, Moreen. You take care too," Thelma says, reaching out here other hand and shaking Moreen's hand. "Thank you for visiting."

"You're welcome and I'll drop that soup off with Bessi, all right?" Moreen asks.

"OK dear," Thelma says, closing her eyes.

"And, I will be back tomorrow morning, if not tonight," Bessi says, kissing Thelma on the forehead.

"Thank you, dear," Thelma says as she watches both Moreen and Bessi leave the room.

Moreen starts crying in the elevator and Bessi tries to comfort her. "Now, now Moreen, at least she is not suffering."

"Oh poor, dear Thelma," Moreen says, wiping her eyes with a handkerchief. "Is she going to make it through this?"

"We don't know yet," Bessi says, rubbing Moreen on her shoulder and arm. "We can all just pray that she doesn't have to suffer."

"Yes, I'll say a prayer for her," Moreen says, stepping out of the elevator. "Thank you, Bessi, for being such a good friend to her."

"Sure," Bessi says with a smile as she walks out to her car. "I look forward to that soup."

"Yes, I'll go home and start on it today," Moreen says as she waves to Bessi as she gets into her car.

Bessi drives home and folds up the extra fabric from the costumes and then she puts her head down on her sewing table and she has a good cry.

After about a half hour, she stops crying and goes into the bathroom to freshen her makeup. She then takes a deep breath and goes back to her sewing room. "I know what I'll do, I'll make Thelma a blouse that she can wear in the hospital."

As she searches through her patterns, she comes across a slip-over blouse that she decides to make. She then pulls out a box from the closet and starts looking though the fabric. "Oh my, I forgot I had this. It will be perfect," She says, pulling out a floral patterned material. "I hope I have enough fabric to make this."

"Hello, Mom," Louisa says as she enters the sewing room.

"Is it that time all ready?" Bessi says, standing up with the fabric in her hand.

"What are you going to make now?" Louisa asks, kissing her mother on the cheek.

"I want to make Thelma a blouse that she can wear in the hospital," Bessi says, sitting down at her sewing table.

"Oh, that is nice of you, Mom," Louisa says. "I just came home to change my shoes for rehearsal."

"OK, dinner is going to be ready around six o'clock," Bessi says, unfolding a paper pattern from a yellow envelope.

"OK, Mom. See ya," Louisa says, leaving the room and going upstairs. After several minutes, she returns. "See you after rehearsals, Mom."

"OK, dear," Bessi says as she lays out the pattern's pieces over the fabric. "This is going to be enough material. Great!"

Several hours pass and everyone comes home for dinner. Bessi updates the family on Thelma's condition and the kids talk about rehearsals. Silus compliments Bessi for being such a good friend to Thelma. Everyone helps clean up after dinner and then the whole family retires early for the night.

The next day, Bessi wakes up tired. She had a dream that bothered her so she couldn't get a good night's sleep.

Lewis greets Bessi in the kitchen. "Good morning, Mom."

"Good morning, dear," Bessi says as she fills the coffeepot with water.

"How did you sleep last night, Mom?" Lewis says as he pours himself a glass of juice.

"I had a dream that bothers me," Bessi says as she grinds some coffee beans. "I woke up from the dream about two thirty and could not get back to sleep."

"What was the dream?" Lewis asks, taking a drink of juice.

"I dreamed that I visited Thelma in a large iris garden with thousands of blossoms. She was dressed up as a nun and we visited while she weeded the garden. She told me that she was going to die soon and for me not to be worried about that because she got to be in this abbey's garden, taking care of the iris flowers for eternity," Bessi says as she wipes a tear from her eyes.

"Wow," Lewis says as he gives his mother a hug.

"Yes, wow," Bessi says as she hugs Lewis. "Now, go get dressed for school."

"OK, Mom," Lewis says as he kisses her on the cheek then leaves the room.

After breakfast, everyone goes on their way for the day. Bessi gets ready to visit Thelma in the hospital. She takes a piece of fabric to show Thelma the material for her new blouse.

"Well, hello there, stranger," Thelma says as Bessi enters into the hospital room.

"Hello, Thelma. How are you doing today?" Bessi asks as she gives Thelma a kiss on the forehead.

"I had a good night's sleep thanks to sleeping medication, so I do feel better than I felt yesterday," Thelma says, sitting up in her bed. "What is that in your hand?"

"Oh, I wanted to show you the fabric I am using for your new blouse," Bessi says, unfolding the fabric and laying it on Thelma's lap.

"Oh my, how pretty," Thelma says with a smile. "You are such a dear friend."

"Well, you are my best friend," Bessi says, patting Thelma on the hand. "Now, the nurse said she will bring in the things needed for a sponge bath. How does that sound?"

"I could use a good rinsing off," Thelma says as she strokes the fabric. "This material has a good feel to it."

"If you remember, that was the fabric I used for *Romeo and Juliet* three years ago," Bessi says, seeing the nurse come into the room with the bathing supplies. "Thank you, Betty."

"You're welcome," the nurse says as she sets the things on the counter and then goes over to the IV machine. "I'll change the IV bag when you're done with your bath."

"Thank you," Thelma says as she pushes off the blanket and sheet.

"Just push the button when you are finished," the nurse says as she leaves the room.

"Bessi, thank you for being such a good friend," Thelma says as she shakes her head. "I don't know what I would do without you."

"I'll get the warm water in the tub if you want to get off your gown," Bessi says as she closes the door to the room.

"The nurse gave me some special soap that won't dry my skin," Thelma says as she takes off her hospital gown.

Bessi gives Thelma a sponge bath. Then Thelma is out of energy and ready for a nap. Bessi changes her sheets and pillowcase then puts her to bed. After leaving the hospital, Bessi goes to the church to see Silus.

"Hello, Silus," Bessi says, entering into the church office.

"Hello, Bessi. Are you OK?" Silus asks, hugging Bessi who starts to cry. "Oh, let it out," he says as she cries on his shoulder while he holds onto her tight. "Are things that bad for Thelma?"

"Yes, and she seems to get worse every day," Bessi says, wiping her tears with Silus' handkerchief. "I had a dream last night that she was going to die soon."

"Well, that was just a dream, honey," Silus says, hugging Bessi again.

"Oh, but, dreams are so much more than you give them credit to be," Bessi says, pulling away and blowing her nose.

"I know you want them to be," Silus says with a smile. "What happened in the dream?"

"Thelma was going to die and be a gardener in an abbey's iris garden," Bessi says, looking up at Silus.

"Well, that would be a good thing, wouldn't it?" Silus asks.

"Yes, I will just miss her, that's all," Bessi says. "I guess it is a better life than suffering with some illness."

"I would hope she doesn't have to suffer any longer," Silus says with a nod of his head. "I am sorry she has this illness and I am sorry that you will lose your best friend."

"Thank you, Silus," Bessi says, taking a deep breath. "Well, I need to get home and finish making her blouse to wear in the hospital instead of the hospital gown."

"That is a nice thing to do for her," Silus says, hugging Bessi again. "OK, I should be home at the regular time, but if you need me, I come home sooner."

"Thank you, honey," Bessi says, stepping away with a wave back to Silus. She then slowly drives over to Thelma's house and checks on the cat Tobu. She feeds him and rubs him all over which is what Thelma used to do all the time. Bessi cries a little more then goes home to work on Thelma's blouse.

Three hours pass before Bessi takes a break and has a cup of tea. She stands looking out her kitchen window at her new dwarf apple tree. After she finishes her tea, she goes back to sewing and finishes the project around four.

Bessi decides to deliver the blouse to Thelma so she drives to the hospital. Several nurses were in Thelma's room and a doctor was listening to her heart through a stethoscope.

"Is she all right?" Bessi whispers to one of the nurses.

"No, she has an infection that is not responding to medication," The nurse says with a shake of her head. "I'll let the doctor talk with you."

"Thank you," Bessi says a she sits in the chair across from Thelma's bed.

"You must be Bessi?" the doctor asks as he shakes her hand. "I am Dr. Wundrig. I will be following Thelma for the duration of her treatment."

"Oh good, how is she doing?" Bessi asks, looking over to Thelma who lays in the bed motionless with her eyes closed.

"She is not responding to medication and she now has three different bacteria in her blood stream that we can't seem to treat. She is very weak. We stopped the radiation for now so that her body will have a better chance at fighting the bacteria. I wish we could do more for her but we can't right now. If she regains her strength and becomes responsive to the medication, then we can start the radiation again. But, for now, we just have to wait," he says as he looks over to Thelma and then leaves the room. The nurses follow him.

"Thanks, doctor, for speaking with me," Bessi says as she steps over to Thelma's bedside and she begins stroking her arm.

"Oh hello, Bessi," Thelma says with a hoarse throat and tired eyes.

"Guess what? I finished the blouse," Bessi says with a smile and teary eyes.

"Oh my, thank you, Bessi," Thelma says, trying to lift her upper body and reposition herself. "Help me put it on, dear."

"Are you sure you feel up to it?" Bessi asks.

"Yes, I would like very much to wear it now," Thelma says, sitting up with Bessi's help. They both work on getting the hospital gown off and Bessi slips the blouse over Thelma's head and arms.

"Oh my, it feels wonderful, Bessi," Thelma says as she leans back onto the bed and takes in a deep breath. "I just love your choice of material."

"Thank you, Thelma. I am so glad you like it," Bessi says as she holds her hand.

"Here, sit down next to me," Thelma says, patting the bed with her other hand. "I am so happy t o see you, Bessi. I feel afraid right now."

"Don't be afraid, Thelma. I'll be here with you as much as you want," Bessi says with teary eyes.

"I know, dear, but, I am afraid all the same," Thelma says. "I have a feeling that I am going to die soon and I fear death."

"Would you like to have Silus come in a talk with you?" Bessi asks, wiping her tears running down her face. She keeps strong and poised as Thelma begins to cry too.

"No, that is OK. I don't want anyone one else to see me like this," Thelma says, wiping her tears with a tissue that Bessi hands her. "I never have really believed in heaven but I sure hope there is a place that we all go to that is good."

"I think you will be going to a very good place and I am sure that you are going to be happy there too," Bessi says, patting her hand lightly. "And, I bet you that there will even be flowers there for you to take care of."

"That would be nice," Thelma says with a smile. "I feel better all ready."

"Me too," Bessi says, wiping her tears and smiling a big wonderful smile.

"I have always loved your smile," Thelma says. "It makes me smile."

"Then I'll smile as much as I can for you," Bessi says with a chuckle. "Well, now I need another sewing project."

"Make Lewis something," Thelma says, breathing heavily.

"That would be a good idea. I could make him a pair of shorts for the summer," Bessi says with a smile. "He already has a bunch of shirts in his closet."

"Make him a pair of shorts with cats on the material," Thelma says with a smile. "Or maybe he would be too embarrassed to wear them in public."

"I'll ask him first, then I'll look in the store catalog for several samples to show him. I like to give him a choice of what I make him," Bessi says softly rubbing Thelma's hand. "I like your idea of the cats."

"How is little Tobu doing on his own?" Thelma asks as she closes her eyes and sets her head back.

"He misses you terribly and is starving for affection so I gave him a good petting today," Bessi says, taking in a deep breath. "Maybe I should bring him home with me until you get better. That way he wouldn't be so alone."

"Would you mind that?" Thelma asks, opening her eyes.

"Not at all. I'll pick him up on the way home tonight," Bessi says with a nod of her head.

"Well, dear, you better run along now and fix dinner for your lovely family."

"OK, if you will be all right?" Bessi asks as she stands up.

"Whatever happens, just remember we are the best of friends," Thelma says as Bessi gives her a kiss on the forehead and a hug.

"I will be in tomorrow to see you OK?" Bessi says as she starts walking toward the door. "Thank you for being my best friend, Thelma."

"You're welcome and thank you for being mine," Thelma says with a smile.

Bessi goes home after picking up Tobu and cooks dinner and talks to the family about friendship and how important it is to have a good friend. She cries a little but is able to hold herself together enough to get through dinner and into bed.

The next morning Bessi is again the first to awake and go downstairs. She gets the coffeepot going and then sits in her sewing room, staring at her sewing machine.

"Good morning, Mom," Lewis says as he passes by the door.

"Good morning, Lewis," Bessi says as she follows him into the kitchen where he gets himself a glass of orange juice. "What did you dream last night?"

"Let's see, I dreamed that I was in a forest wandering with my sewing basket. As I was walking, I kept wondering why I was there. I suddenly heard whispering through the soft breeze. An old tree began talking to me. He told me that he was going to die soon and wanted me to sew his leaves back onto his branches before he died. I told him I would, so I collected a bunch of leaves. I climbed the tree and began sewing the leaves back on to the branches. The tree then started weeping with joy and then died. His spirit swept past me as the soft breeze carried it away. He thanked me and then I woke up," Bessi says, taking in a deep breath.

"Wow, Mom, you have the best dreams," Lewis says, shaking his head. "I just dreamed that I was in a football game and I kept running for the ball and never caught it," he says, taking another drink of juice.

"Oh my," Bessi says, rubbing the top of his head. "I'm sort of glad that I had my dream instead of yours."

"I wish I would have had your dream. It sounded really neat and spiritual," Lewis says as he walks over to the sink drinking the rest of his juice.

"What would you like for breakfast?" Bessi asks.

"How about poached eggs over toast," Lewis says as he rinses his glass.

"All right, poached eggs it will be," Bessi says with a smile. "Now, go get dressed and I'll call you when breakfast is ready."

"OK, Mom. I am getting excited. It is only two more days until the play," Lewis says, exiting the kitchen.

Bessi prepares breakfast and everyone eats then goes about their day. After she cleans up the kitchen, she waters the patio plants and her dwarf apple tree, then heads off to the hospital.

Thelma is sleeping when she gets there so she sits in the chair and watches her sleep. After about an hour, Thelma wakes and sees Bessi sitting there staring out the window.

"Oh hello, Bessi. How long have you been waiting?" Thelma asks as she repositions herself on the bed.

"Not long, I just didn't want to awake you," Bessi says, approaching the bed and softly gripping Thelma's hand. "How are you today?"

"Not good. I am very weak and tired, and I just don't feel good," Thelma says, taking a deep breath. "I wish there was something they could do for me."

"Me too, dear," Bessi says, sitting on the bed next to Thelma. "Have you seen the doctor yet today?"

"Yes, he was in early this morning doing his rounds," Thelma says. "He said I was getting worse every day. I knew that."

"I am sorry to hear that," Bessi says, shaking her head. "Do you feel up to a sponge bath today?"

"Oh, maybe later in the day, and, you don't have to bother with it. The nurse's aide can do it," Thelma says, closing her eyes. "I don't mean to sound like I don't want you to do it, it is just that I don't want you to feel like it is something you have to do."

"It is something I am glad to help you with," Bessi says with a smile.

"Well, I'll let you only if you really want too," Thelma says, patting Bessi's hand. "But, let's do it later when I have more energy."

"OK, I'll run my errands, then pick up some food for Tobu and take it to my house. I'll come back later, OK?" Bessi asks as she sees the nurse enter into the room.

The nurse checks the IV fluids and asks Thelma how she feels. She then leaves.

Bessi then goes off on her errands and gets the cat food to take home with her. She returns to the hospital and gives Thelma her sponge bath. Thelma is getting worse and weaker. She can barely sit up and insists on wearing the new blouse that Bessi made for her.

The rest of the day is full of events for everyone. The kids are excited about the play and Silus is busy with the church and several protesters that say they are going to picket the play's opening night.

The next day, the day before the play, Thelma takes a turn for the worse and goes into a coma. Bessi sits by her side holding her hand and talking to her. The day passes and the nurse convinces Bessi that nothing can be done for Thelma now.

Bessi goes home and is comforted by her family. After dinner, they all have a family meeting about Thelma's condition and its effect on Bessi. The kids are very supportive and they all huddle together as Bessi has a good cry.

The next day, the day of the play, the kids are overexcited and Silus is very busy. He is trying to calm a handful of members that teamed up with the other church to picket in front of the school.

The day passes and it is several hours until the play starts. All the students are in their costumes and Bessi is busy making last minute alterations. Silus is in front with the protesters trying to get them to go home or come in and watch the play.

Bessi gets a phone call at the school that Thelma has passed away. She hears the news and starts crying. Several minutes pass and she pulls herself together, continuing to prepare the kids for the play.

The play begins even with the protesters outside. Most of the town attends and the play is a success. The students get a standing ovation and are proud of their performance.

After the play, Silus, Bessi, Louisa, and Lewis all drive to a restaurant to eat dinner . The kids are still in their costumes and half of the class ends up in the same place to eat. The atmosphere is full of energy as they all celebrate their play.

On the way home, Silus tells the three of them that he is very proud of them and that he loves them dearly. Bessi thanks him and tells him she is proud to be his wife and their mother. She then tells everyone that Thelma passed away just before the play.

Lewis is the first to say something meaningful and Louisa does the same. Silus comforts her as several tears fall from her face.

"At least she doesn't have to suffer any longer, and she gets to be with her flowers in a garden fit for eternity." Bessi says taking in a deep breath.

The End

978-0-595-36959-1
0-595-36959-6

Printed in the United States
38268LVS00005B

9 780595 369591